MW01592861

THE AMISH DREAM

THE AMISH QUILTING CIRCLE

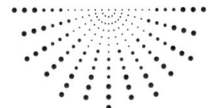

SARAH MILLER
IRENE GLICK

SWEETBOOKHUB.COM

WELCOME TO THE AMISH QUILTING CIRCLE

What is more lovely than a quilting circle? Good friends getting together to drink coffee, eat cake, talk and work on a quilt or two. It is a wonderful way to spend an afternoon being both productive and having fun.

Only, this quilting circle likes to do a little matchmaking along with the quilting.

Join the ladies of Faith's Creek as they see who they will match next.

All the books are sweet and family friendly with no nasty suprises.

If you missed the first book, you can grab An Englischer's Folly here.

If you are not already a member of my readers newsletter, join here, for free, to be the first to find out when new books are released and for occasional free content.

CHAPTER ONE

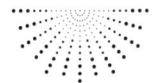

FAITH'S CREEK, PENNSYLVANIA.

There were three dozen eggs that afternoon and a dozen from the ducks. Sadie Erb was busy collecting them and checking that none of them were broken. She would box them up and sell them in her stall at the market. The hens clucked around her feet and the ducks quacked in the little pond she had built for them at the far end of the garden. It was an idyllic scene, the sun was shining, and Sadie was humming happily to herself.

"Another night the fox didn't get you," she said, for Sadie was always worried about foxes.

Her flock was forty-strong, and she had twelve prized ducks, too. Sadie loved animals and was happiest out on the smallholding behind the house she shared with her *daed*, Leroy. It was a simple life, but the two of them got by. Sadie grew vegetables, too, and on a Tuesday and Friday, she sold her produce – including the eggs – at the market in Faith's Creek. Her *daed* had been unwell for some time and could not help her as he used to. The responsibility of looking after them was now Sadie's, and she took it very seriously.

"Come on now, get pecking," she said, throwing feed across the small enclosure where the hens and ducks roamed during the day.

Leroy had built the hen house for her and fenced in a small patch at the end of the garden with chicken wire some five years ago when his health had allowed him to do more on the smallholding. There was a gate with a latch, and having fed the chickens and ducks, Sadie stepped back out into the vegetable patch, closing the gate behind her, and securing it.

"You all be *gut* now," she said, smiling at the sight of the chickens and ducks pecking at the feed.

There were too many to give each a name, but most she recognized by their personality. There was the small one with white feathers and red specks that always seemed to hold back shyly, and the large one who strutted like a cockerel and always seemed to push towards the front. The ducks, too, had their individual traits, and two in particular always went around as a pair, like twins. Sadie could happily have watched them for hours, even as she knew she had chores to see to.

"Did you get many eggs today?" a familiar voice called out across the garden.

Sadie turned to find her *grossmammi*, Mary Erb, watching her from the gate that led out onto the road in front of the house.

"Three dozen, and a dozen from the ducks. Do you want any?" she asked.

Mary unlatched the gate and stepped into the garden. She was a small woman with cropped gray hair and a wrinkled face. She wore a plain white dress, shawl, and *kapp* in the traditional style, and was carrying a basket of knitting – Mary was always knitting, quilting, sewing, or making something. Sadie was wearing a shawl that her *grossmammi* had made her as a birthday present at that very moment, and not a month went by when Mary did not present her with something she had made or mended or thrifted.

"You keep your eggs. You need to make money from them, not give them away," Mary said, smiling at her.

Sadie set down her basket and went to meet her at the gate. "Have you been to the quilting circle?" she asked, and Mary nodded.

"I've just come from there. I'm making a quilt for Naomi's baby," she replied, and she reached into her basket and pulled out a small blanket embroidered with teddy bears in brown felt with black eyes.

Sadie had been pleased to hear the news of the arrival of Naomi Wittmer's baby after her marriage to Aaron Wittmer the previous year. He was called Lucas, and Sadie knew that Mary had a soft spot for him. She was always talking about him – the implication being she would like a *grosskinner* of her own.

"How's she doing? I haven't seen her for a few weeks. Is she still making cakes?" Sadie asked.

She knew Naomi vaguely, they had been at school together, though Naomi was a year older than Sadie, and whilst the two of them were acquainted they were not close friends.

"She's doing well. She manages the business with Serena's help. She takes care of Lucas during the day when Naomi's busy making cakes," Mary replied.

Serena was Aaron's *mamm*, a woman who had once confined herself almost entirely to the house and had been known for being something of a hypochondriac. But the arrival of the *boppli* had changed that, and Sadie would often see her walking proudly along the road towards Faith's Creek, pushing the pram containing little Lucas.

"I'm glad they're doing well. It's a lovely blanket," Sadie said.

Mary nodded and raised her right eyebrow. "I'd like a chance to make one for your *boppli* one day," she replied.

Sadie smiled. In recent months, her *grossmammi* had been far more vocal about the prospects of her getting married. Sadie had just turned twenty, and whilst she did not consider herself to be in any hurry to get married, it seemed those around her did, for her *daed* had expressed a similar sentiment.

"It's not quite as easy as that," Sadie said.

They had stepped up onto the porch at the side of the house now, and Sadie sat down on the swing chair with a sigh.

"Aren't you looking for a husband, Sadie?" Mary asked.

Sadie was *not* looking for a husband. She had tried – albeit half-heartedly – and at the games night in the Hochstettler barn just last month she had spoken at length to Reuben Stein who had seemed very interested in everything she had to say. Unfortunately, Reuben was interested in what most women had to say, and Sadie had discovered he was happily engaged in a round of "talking" before settling on one particular woman: Anne Bontrager, with whom Sadie believed she could never compete.

"Am I meant to be? I've got enough chores to see to here without thinking about a husband," she replied.

It was true, Sadie was always busy, and with her *daed's* condition deteriorating, she knew her responsibilities would only grow. She had her hens and ducks to see to. Then there was the garden itself, where weeds sprang up overnight, and there was always something to harvest or tend. She had her market stall, and there the house, not to mention taking care of her *daed*. With so many burdens to bear, Sadie had little time for anything more, let alone the business of finding a husband.

"Oh, Sadie. It's what you need. You can't stay like this forever. You can't just grow into an old maid. Don't you want a husband?" Mary asked, looking at her with a pained expression on her face.

"It's not that I don't want a husband, it's just... well, it's not as easy as that. I've never been asked to step out by anyone. I always feel shy," Sadie replied, and Mary tutted.

"If you think that, you'll believe it. But you're a pretty young woman, Sadie. You don't need to be shy. You've got lots going for you. Any man would be proud to have you on his arm and call you his *fraa*," she said.

Sadie smiled. She knew her *grossmammi* was only trying to lift her spirits. Sadie *had* thought a lot about husbands recently. She guessed that she was an attractive enough young woman, even as she played down her looks. Her hair was long and dark and stayed well beneath her *kapp*, her eyes were a deep blue, and her cheeks were rosy. She was slim, and always dressed neatly and modestly. Her interests were varied – she played the usual games and could sing – but somehow, none of this had so far attracted anything more than mere conversation.

"If you say so," Sadie replied, rising to her feet.

She had chores to see to, and like it or not, she had to do them. There was no time to feel sorry for herself or lament about not having a queue of young men looking to court her.

"I do say so, and it's about time we did something about it," Mary said.

Sadie had heard that tone before. When her *grossmammi* got an idea into her head that was it. There would be no stopping her determination now, and Sadie could not help but feel a certain sense of trepidation at the prospect of what would happen next.

"But what can anyone do? You can't force someone to fall in love with you and marry you," Sadie replied.

"Nee, but I can think of something almost as *gut.* The quilting circle. It was us who brought Naomi and Aaron together, and we can do the same for you," Sadie's *grossmammi* said.

There was a triumphant look on her face as though she had settled on a decisive plan.

Sadie shook her head. "I haven't got time to sit making quilts," she said.

Mary smiled and shook her head. "You leave the quilt making to me. It's not the quilts that are important, it's what the others can help with that matters. Between us, we know almost everyone in Faith's Creek. If I can't find you a husband on my own, I know the others can help," she said, still with a look of triumph etched across her face.

Sadie smiled. There was no point in arguing, but now she heard violent coughing from the house. Her *daed* was having one of his fits, and bidding her *grossmammi* goodbye, Sadie hurried into the house. The matter of finding a husband could wait...

CHAPTER TWO

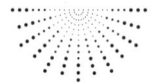

*L*loyd Fehr was trying to catch Fletch, but the dog was having far too much fun running around the garden. He seemed to think it was a game, one which Lloyd was enthusiastically playing, even as he now called out in exasperation to the dog to come to heel.

"Sit, *gut* boy, sit," he said, pointing his finger at Fletch, who paused for a moment and tilted his head to one side, before dashing to the left and then to the right.

He was a cross breed with brown and white shaggy fur – though which breeds and how many crosses were indiscernible, there was no denying that Fletch was cute. Lloyd had raised him from a puppy and had chosen him from a litter belonging to Doctor Yoder, Faith's Creek's resident physician. That had been five years ago, and the two of them had been the closest of companions ever since.

"Is he giving you the runaround?" Lloyd's *mamm*, Melanie, asked.

She had just emerged into the garden from the side door of the house and was carrying a bag of dog treats. At the sight of her, Fletch paused, his body quivering, his nose pointed forwards, and Lloyd laughed.

"I think he knows what's coming," he said as Fletch now rolled obediently onto his back and waggled his legs in the air.

Melanie tossed him a dog treat, and Fletch barked and snatched it up, chewing it down before sitting stock still on the grass, as though his prior exuberance had not occurred.

"I spoil him, I suppose," Melanie said, shaking her head.

"You do. That's why he's so unruly. He's learned he doesn't have to behave unless he gets a reward at the end of it. But at least I can catch him for his walk," Lloyd replied, and Fletch now allowed a lead to be clipped to his collar, standing up obediently as Lloyd beckoned him to follow.

"Are you going down to the creek?" Melanie asked, but Lloyd shook his head.

"I want to go up onto the ridge. I like the view from there. You can see the whole of Faith's Creek. We'll be back later. Come on, Fletch, I'll race you," Lloyd said, and he set off at a run, keeping tight hold of Fletch's lead as they chased together out of the garden and along the track which led from their house across the cornfields.

It was a hot, sunny day, and the sky was blue and clear as Lloyd and Fletch raced along the track. Lloyd was always happiest when he was with Fletch. He was his best friend, and the two of them were inseparable, even as Lloyd had so far failed to train his dog in even the most basic of commands. Still, Lloyd felt his companion always knew how he was feeling. When his mood was low, Fletch was there to comfort him, and when he felt happy, it was as though Fletch felt happy, too.

"This way, boy, along the road, then we'll take the path up to the ridge," Lloyd said, and he pulled at Fletch's lead, the two of them running together around the corner in the road where they almost collided with a young woman carrying a basket.

"Oh... I'm sorry," she exclaimed, looking up from her thoughts with a startled expression on her face.

Lloyd pulled Fletch up, for the dog had leaped at the woman thinking she wanted to play.

"*Nee*, it's me that should be sorry. Come along, Fletch, get back, will you? The lady doesn't want to play," he said, but the woman had set down her basket and was now fondling Fletch's ears – it seemed she was only too happy to play...

"It's all right. I love dogs. I love all animals. What's his name?" she asked, ruffling Fletch's ears.

Fletch loved to have his ears played with, and he sank to the ground with a happy whimper, stretching his front paws out as Lloyd laughed.

"He's Fletch. You've certainly got a way with dogs. He doesn't usually do that for anyone but my *mamm* and I," he said, impressed at the woman's ability to subdue his usually boisterous dog.

"I don't know. I... well, I've got hens and ducks. They're not exactly the same. But when you spend your time around animals, I think you get to know how to handle them. They've all their own personalities," she replied.

Lloyd nodded. He liked the way she spoke. He had ambitions to be a vet and wanted to work with farm animals. He was a carpenter by trade and had a workshop behind his *mamm's* house, but every evening, he would sit down to study and was hoping to enter a correspondence course that summer to learn the necessary science he needed for veterinary school.

"I couldn't agree more. I've had Fletch since he was a puppy, and I know him just as well as he knows me," Lloyd replied, glancing down at Fletch, who was still enjoying having his ears ruffled.

The young woman looked up at Lloyd and smiled. He recognized her vaguely. She had a stall in the market where she sold eggs and vegetables, but he could not remember her name.

"He's lovely. I wish I had a dog. We've got chickens and ducks, and a cat that lives with us when it chooses, but no dog. You're very lucky. He's the perfect companion," she said, patting Fletch on the head and rising to her feet.

"We're just off for a walk on the ridge. We go up there, or down to the creek. I take him every day when I finish work. I'm a carpenter and he likes to sit and watch me work," Lloyd said.

He was surprised how easily he found himself talking to the woman. But that was the advantage of having a dog.

They provided a talking point, and any awkward silence could be filled with further comments on the dog's behavior or personality.

"I might have to persuade my *daed* to get one. He needs a companion around the house, too," the woman said.

"Look, I'm sorry. I didn't introduce myself. I'm Lloyd – Lloyd Fehr. I live on the far side of the cornfield. I recognize you, but I'm sorry, I don't remember your name," he said.

The woman smiled, and it was the sort of smile that lit up a person's face and radiated with warmth.

"I'm Sadie – Sadie Erb. We were probably at school together," she said, and Lloyd nodded.

He remembered her now. They *had* been at school together, though Lloyd was a few years older than Sadie and he could not remember ever having spoken to her before.

"I do remember you. It's nice to meet you. I won't keep you, though. It looks like you're off on an errand," Lloyd said, glancing at Sadie's basket, which contained several boxes of eggs.

"I'm taking duck eggs to the Beiler's house. Sarah Beiler makes the most delicious cakes with them. She always drops a slice off for my *daed*. He's not well at the moment and he doesn't get out much – but he still likes a slice of cake," Sadie replied.

Lloyd smiled.

"Don't let Fletch hear you say the word cake. He once ate a whole seed cake my *mamm* had just baked. I say "ate" – he just buried his nose in it and left a great big hole. The birds enjoyed it," he said, glancing at Fletch, who was now sniffing around in the nearby hedge and pulling on his lead.

"Oh, my – it sounds like nothing's safe when Fletch is around. Anyway, I'd better go. It was nice meeting you – and Fletch," she said and giving the dog a final ruffle behind the ears, she went off along the road, glancing back and waving to them both.

Fletch looked up at Lloyd and put his head on one side.

"What's that expression supposed to mean?" Lloyd asked, raising his eyebrows, but as they walked on, Lloyd could not get the thought of his encounter with Sadie out of his mind.

She had certainly taken to Fletch, and he wondered if the two of them might see one another again. It had been a long time since Lloyd had had such thoughts about a woman. He had been content getting on with his life and letting fate take its course. His carpentry work, his studies, and his dog took up most of his time, but now he wondered if fate had placed something new in his path.

"You've just missed Anna Troyer," Lloyd's *mamm* said when he arrived back from his walk with Fletch.

"Oh, I'm sorry. Did she want something?" Lloyd asked as he undid the lead from Fletch's collar.

"She's got some carpentry jobs for you to do. She said the banister on her stairs is all rotten – wood worm, she thinks – and she wondered if you'd come and put in new spokes. I said you'd be happy to. She was wondering if you could go on Thursday. I said *jah*. Is that all right?" Melanie asked.

"*Jah, Mamm*, I can go on Thursday. It won't be a problem. Troyer... that was Naomi Wittmer's maiden name, wasn't it?" Lloyd asked, trying to recall something of the many ways in which the population of Faith's Creek was connected.

"She's Naomi's aunt. She's a nice person. I see her at the market sometimes, and it was nice of her to think of you. I'm so proud of you, Lloyd. You work so hard to make a living," Melanie said, and Lloyd smiled.

"It's all for a reason, *Mamm,*" he replied, thinking of how proud he would feel when at last he had realized his dreams, even as the road to get there was still a long one.

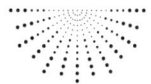

CHAPTER THREE

Sadie's *daed* was coughing. He coughed a lot, but today he seemed worse. Sadie had brought him a glass of water and was rubbing his back as he sat forward in his chair by the stove. His face was pale and his whole body was convulsing as he coughed.

"Oh, *Daed*. Shall I fetch Doctor Yoder? You can't go on like this," Sadie said, but her *daed* shook his head.

"*Nee*... I don't need... *nee*, not the doctor," he said, and taking a heavy breath, he sat back in his chair with a sigh.

Sadie knew her *daed* was unwilling to admit the severity of his condition. He hid it, not only from others but from himself, too. Sadie would hear him coughing at night, and the more he coughed, the more she worried.

"But you're getting worse, *Daed*," she said.

"I'm fine. I just needed some water. There... I feel better now," he said, looking up at her with a forced smile on his face.

Sadie knew there was little point in arguing with him. Her *daed* was stubborn, and once he had made up his mind, that was that.

"Shall I get you another glass?" she asked, but he shook his head.

"I need some fresh air. Help me out onto the porch, will you?" he said, and with some difficulty, Sadie was able to support him up from his chair and out onto the porch, where they sat on the swing chair together.

It was a warm day, and the ducks were splashing about in the pond at the end of the run, whilst the chickens were scratching in the ground. Sadie had been busy working in the garden that morning, and she had pulled up dozens of beets, which now lay tied in bunches drying in the sunshine.

"Do you like the looks of the beets, *Daed*? They'll sell well in the market stall, I'm sure," Sadie said.

"You work hard, Sadie. You always have done. I'm proud of you," he said, and Sadie smiled.

She had lost her *mamm* when she was very young, and without siblings, it had just been her and her *daed* taking care of the smallholding together. They had their disagreements at times, but Sadie had always known she was loved, and that her *daed* wanted what was best for her.

"I'll sow some more, and cabbages, too. Everyone likes cabbages," Sadie said.

Her *daed* nodded as a ponderous look came over his face. Sadie knew what was coming.

"There's more to life than cabbages, though, Sadie. I've been thinking..." he began, but Sadie interrupted him.

"Are you going to tell me to get married? You're just like *grossmammi*," she said, and her *daed* smiled.

"She wants what's best for you, too," he replied.

Sadie sighed. "I'm happy, *Daed*. You don't need to worry about me," she said, but he shook his head.

"But I do worry about you. I'm not well, Sadie. We both know that. I know I don't admit it, and that's my own stupid fault. But when my time comes, I don't want to think I've failed you and left you alone," he said.

Sadie took his hand in hers and shook her head. He had been the best of *daeds* to her and she loved him dearly. The thought of losing him brought tears to her eyes, and she shook her head and brought his hand to her lips.

"You're not going anywhere soon, *Daed*. Just let Doctor Yoder have a proper look at you, that's all," she said.

"Forget Doctor Yoder. It's you I'm worried about, and so is your *grossmammi*. We want what's best for you, Sadie, and what's best for you is to get married. You need a man to take care of you and to help you with the smallholding," he said, with a definite tone in his voice.

Sadie did not need a man to take care of her – nor to help her on the smallholding. She knew as much as any man about growing vegetables, tilling the soil, and taking care of her animals – more than most men, in fact.

"I don't. I know what I'm doing..." she began.

The conversation always went this way, and Sadie would insist she had everything under control, even as she knew there were times when she struggled. But today, it seemed her *daed* had something more in mind.

"I know you do, but that's not the point. You need a husband, Sadie, and I've found just the man for you," he said.

Sadie was not expecting this. Her *daed's* words on marriage usually ended at the insistence of necessity rather than a practical solution. Only once had he urged her to consider a possible candidate, and that man had been discovered to be courting another woman. Sadie looked at her *daed* in surprise.

"What do you mean?" she asked.

"I mean, Samuel Miller, Dwain's son. He'd be just right for you," her *daed* replied, but Sadie made a face.

Samuel Miller – the son of Dwain Miller, a friend of Sadie's *daed* – was a man she was glad to have little to do with. He was twenty-five and worked as a mechanic. But the Millers were incomers, Englischers from Oregon who had moved to Faith's Creek when Samuel was a *kinner*.

Sadie knew Samuel detested Faith's Creek and its way of life. He spoke disparagingly of the people and always made sure anyone who spoke to him knew he intended to leave the community as soon as he had saved up enough money for a property bond somewhere far away. Was her *daed* serious? Did he really think his friend's son was a suitable match?

"Samuel Miller? Are you serious?" she asked.

Leroy nodded. "I spoke to Dwain about it yesterday. He thinks you and Samuel need to spend some time together – to get to know one another," he replied.

Sadie shook her head. She had no intention of getting to know Samuel Miller, and she certainly had no intention of marrying him, either.

"I'm going for a walk," she said, rising to her feet.

"Think about it, Sadie. Don't dismiss the idea out of hand. I said you'd meet him today. He's going to come here this afternoon. Don't be late back," he called after her.

Sadie hurried across the garden and out of the gate onto the road. She was making for her *grossmammi's* house, her mind filled with conflicting thoughts. As she walked past the turning onto the path up to the ridge, she thought of her encounter with Lloyd Fehr and his dog. The thought made her smile – despite the sorry situation she now found herself in.

"I can't marry a man like Samuel Miller," she told herself, shaking her head in grim determination.

Her *grossmammi* was sympathetic, even as she herself had been part of the plan.

"I want you to get married, Sadie. That's no secret. But I don't know if I like the idea of you marrying the son of an Englischer. He's always telling everyone how much he hates Faith's Creek, isn't he? Why does he want to marry an Amish woman, if that's the case?" she said, shaking her head as she poured out a cup of coffee for Sadie.

"I don't know. I don't want to know. But I'm not going to marry him," Sadie replied, folding her arms defiantly.

"Your *daed* just wants what's best for you. He's got it into his mind he needs to do something before... it's too late," she said, shaking her head sadly.

She was Sadie's *daed's mamm*, and Sadie had often spoken to her of how worried she was at the prospect of her *daed's* condition growing worse. She could not imagine her life without him, and it seemed he was planning for the very worst.

"But he doesn't have to. And he certainly doesn't have to if he thinks I'll be happy with a man like that. I've barely spoken two words to him in my entire life, and those were enough. He's coming to the house, apparently. I'll have to put him off somehow. But the question won't go away. My *daed* won't rest until I'm married," Sadie said, shaking her head sadly.

"Well... that's where I might be able to help you, Sadie. Won't you come to the quilting circle with me on Thursday? It'll do you *gut*. You never do anything for yourself. All you do is work. I'd like it. I'd like to spend time with you, and the other women would like it, too. I don't know if Naomi's going to be there, but it'll take your mind off things for a while, don't you think?" she said.

Sadie nodded. Her *grossmammi* was right. She *did* need something to take her mind off the thought of Samuel Miller. She knew nothing about sewing or embroidery, but the thought of doing something different appealed to her, and she nodded.

"All right, I'll come," she said, and her *grossmammi* smiled.

"That's wonderful, Sadie. You never know... we might help you in just the way we helped Naomi," she replied, and despite Sadie's misgivings, she wondered if the quilting circle might be able to do something to save her from her *daed's* misguided plans.

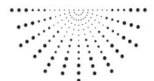

CHAPTER FOUR

"**C**ome on, Fletch. Don't dawdle. We've got work to do," Lloyd said, as he pulled on Fletch's lead.

The dog looked at him as though to ask why they were going out for their walk in the morning, rather than the evening.

"Oh, you're wondering if you're getting two walks today, are you? We're not going far. Just to Anna Troyer's house. You can play in her garden for the morning whilst I see to this banister," Lloyd said.

He was carrying his carpentry bag and some pieces of wood tied up with a cord and he whistled as he walked along. Lloyd usually worked in his workshop, but he was happy to accept the commission from Anna, hoping it might lead to further work from her friends and acquaintances.

"Oh, there you are. I'm pleased to see you, and right on time, too," Anna said, as she answered the door to Lloyd a few moments later.

"Good morning. Would you mind if I tied my dog up outside whilst I work? He'll be happy in the shade of the porch. He won't dig up any of your flowers, I promise," Lloyd said, glancing around him at Anna's immaculately neat garden, but his employer would not hear of it.

"Bring him inside, I love dogs. And the ladies from the quilting circle will love him, too," she said.

Lloyd looked at her in surprise. He was not used to working in front of an audience.

"Oh, I'm sorry. I didn't realize you had company," he said, but Anna shook her head.

"They'll not be here until eleven o'clock. We meet every Thursday to quilt. We're quite harmless, so don't look so worried," she said, beckoning Lloyd – and Fletch – into the house.

Lloyd was a naturally shy person. It was one of the reasons he liked animals so much. Animals were content to keep a person company without demanding anything in return. They did not need conversation, nor did they create atmospheres, or have expectations. Animals just were, and Lloyd liked that. Carpentry, too, was a solitary job, and Lloyd would happily spend the whole day in his workshop without seeing anyone, and with only Fletch for company.

"I'm sure I can get everything finished by eleven o'clock. It's just the spokes, isn't it? In the banister, I mean," Lloyd asked, taking his work boots off on the mat.

The parlor was arranged for a meeting with comfortable chairs placed in a semi-circle. There were plates of cakes on a table in the middle of the room, and a large basket contained a pile of blankets and half-finished pieces of embroidery so that the scene was set for the quilting circle.

"Don't worry at all. I should've had this seen to months ago, but I kept putting it off. I was so pleased to overhear your *mamm* in the grocery store talking to Sarah Beiler. She's so proud of you. She was talking about your carpentry work and that's what got me thinking – so I called around to see you – well, your *mamm* – and here you are," Anna said.

Lloyd smiled and nodded.

"I'm happy to help," he said, turning now to the banister.

Lloyd could see the offending spokes clearly enough. Three of them had woodworm and it would be a simple enough task to cut them out and replace the spokes with new joins. Fletch was – to Lloyd's immense relief – behaving himself well. It was as though he realized he had to, and Anna had put down a bowl of water for him to lap.

"And I've got plenty of other jobs for you, if you want them, that is," Anna said, smiling at Lloyd, who nodded.

He was used to turning his hand to all manner of different carpentry tasks. He made pieces of furniture, fitted floorboards, repaired broken hinges, and made all manner of useful things in his workshop.

"That's very kind, *denke*. This shouldn't be a difficult job. I'll get started right away," he said, unbundling the wood and taking some measurements.

Lloyd was a steady worker and once he began a task, he saw it through to the end.

"Would you like a slice of banana loaf?" Anna asked, appearing from the kitchen with another plate of cakes – it was looking like not so much a quilting circle but a tea party.

Lloyd's *mamm* was an excellent baker, but it seemed Anna was, too – or perhaps this was Naomi's doing.

"It's delicious," he said, as Fletch eyed him longingly.

He had almost finished repairing the rotten banisters and was beginning to clear up the mess of sawdust and wood shavings when a knock came at the door.

"Here's the first of them," Anna said, hurrying to open the door.

Lloyd recognized the first arrival as Rebecca Kuhns, a friend of his *mamm*, and she greeted him warmly, commenting on the excellence of his work and suggesting she, too, could find plenty of jobs for Lloyd to do.

"It's so difficult to find a reliable tradesman," she commented, helping herself to a piece of banana bread before sitting down on a chair in the semi-circle.

Lloyd did not want to remain longer than was necessary and he swiftly finished tidying up and had just packed up his carpentry bag when a second knock came at the door. Anna went to answer it, and Lloyd was surprised – though not unhappy – to see Sadie Erb standing on the porch. He had not realized she was a member of the quilting circle – though there was no reason why he should – and she was accompanied by her *grossmammi*, Mary Erb, who greeted Lloyd warmly.

"I'm glad she's finally getting those banisters seen to. If she ever had a fall, she'd go straight through them," she said, glancing at Anna, who smiled.

Fletch had recognized his ear-ruffling friend, and he went over to Sadie and began to make a fuss of her.

"Hello, Fletch. You're a *gut* dog, aren't you?" she said, kneeling to pet him.

"You've met before, I see," Anna said, glancing at Lloyd, who blushed.

"We bumped into one another whilst I was taking Fletch for his walk the other day. It's... nice to see you again, Sadie," he said.

Sadie smiled. "It's nice to see you, too," she replied, holding his gaze with her large, deep blue eyes.

"I'm pleased you've joined us, Sadie. You'll not be on your own. Naomi's coming today and she's bringing Lucas, too," Anna said, as Sadie rose to her feet.

"I persuaded her to come... she's been a bit upset," Mary said, and Sadie shot her an exasperated look

"*Grossmammi...*" she began, glancing at Lloyd and blushing.

"It's no secret, Sadie. It's your *daed* that's upset you. He wants her to marry Samuel Miller – the Englishcher's son," Mary continued.

At these words, Lloyd's heart skipped a beat. He had not realized Sadie was courting, and he suddenly felt terribly foolish for allowing himself to get carried away over idle fantasies. Since they had met on the road, Lloyd had thought a lot about Sadie. She was pretty, that much was certain, but it was her love for animals and her kindness to Fletch which had attracted him more. If Fletch had taken a liking to Sadie, then Lloyd could not help doing so, too.

"Samuel Miller? Isn't he the one that's always bad-mouthing Faith's Creek to anyone who'll listen?" Rebecca said.

"That's right, he's forever saying bad things about the community. He wants to leave as soon as he can and move back to Oregon – that's where they're from. I don't know why you'd ever consider marrying him," Anna said.

Lloyd took this as the right time to leave. He cleared his throat and Fletch came to his side.

"I'll be going now. Just let me know about those other jobs. I'll be happy to come back," he said.

Anna smiled at him, but Sadie looked embarrassed, and Lloyd was only too glad to be back outside on the porch in the sunshine. He could not understand why Sadie would even consider marrying a man like Samuel Miller. He knew him by reputation, and he knew he had no love for Faith's Creek or its way of life.

"Does she really want to marry a man like that? Will her daed make her?" he wondered to himself as he returned home.

Fletch was trotting happily at his heels and he looked down at him and sighed.

"I suppose I shouldn't have jumped to conclusions, should I, Fletch?" he said, and the dog barked.

But try as he might, Lloyd could not get the thought of Sadie and what she was doing out of his mind, and the more he thought of her in the coming days, the stronger his feelings grew...

CHAPTER FIVE

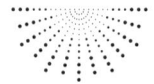

"... *A*nd pull through and up, down, and pull through and up, down..." that's it, you're getting it. Don't worry, I was all fingers and thumbs when I started. You'll soon get the hang of it," Naomi Wittmer said.

She was helping Sadie with the first patch of a quilt, and Sadie, having only ever stitched a button on one of her *daed's* shirts, was finding it difficult. The other women were sitting effortlessly, talking, stitching, and drinking coffee. Sarah Beiler had arrived shortly after Lloyd had left, accompanied by Susanna Bontrager, and Naomi, so that the quilting circle was complete. They were all working on their own projects, and Naomi had encouraged Sadie to begin her own quilt, just as she had done on the first day she had attended the quilting circle over a year ago.

"I don't know if I'll ever be able to do it," Sadie said, and Naomi smiled.

"You'll get there. I was just the same as you. I couldn't even thread the needle, let alone make it sew a pattern. But bit by bit, I got there. I made Lucas a quilt, and now I'm making him some clothes for when he gets a little bigger," Naomi said.

Lucas was lying peacefully in a basket at her side. He had been asleep the whole time, but now he stirred and wriggled, uttering a cry, and opening his eyes.

"Have we got ourselves a new member?" Anna said, smiling down at her great nephew as Naomi lifted Lucas out and held him in her arms.

"He's getting bigger by the day. It won't be long before he'll be sitting up on his own. I don't know where the time goes," Naomi said.

"Why don't you let Sadie hold him? I think she'd like a break from quilting for a few minutes," Anna said.

Sadie was about to protest. She knew nothing about *bopplis*, but Naomi seemed relieved at the suggestion and promptly handed Lucas to Sadie, who cradled him in her arms. Her *grossmammi* cooed at her.

"Oh, Sadie, you look just right holding a *boppli*. It won't be long until you have one of your own," she said, and Sadie blushed.

Lucas looked up at her and smiled a toothless grin. He was a dear little thing, with a wisp of black hair and wide, blue eyes.

"But not by Samuel Miller, I hope. You're not seriously entertaining the idea of marrying him, are you?" Anna asked.

Sadie shook her head. "*Nee...* I'm not. But it's my *daed*, he... he's ill, and he's not getting any better. He thinks I need a husband. He thinks I need to be taken care of," she replied, and the other women glanced at one another and shook their heads.

"I'm not sure about Samuel Miller," Sarah Beiler said, shaking her head. "He's always got a criticism about our way of life. He doesn't like living here, that's for certain."

"I know, I don't understand my *daed*." Sadie felt helpless. She had endured an uncomfortable meeting with Samuel, during which he had spoken almost entirely about himself and his ambitions. He had told her that taking care of hens and tending a small-holding held no interest for him and that any wife of his would be expected to do a great deal more. He had done nothing to change Sadie's prior opinion of him – if anything, their brief encounter had only strengthened it.

"I agree. Isn't there something you can do, Mary?" Anna asked, turning to Sadie's *grossmammi*, who nodded.

"Well... I was rather hoping we might all do something. Didn't we help Naomi find her husband? And look how happy they are together," she said.

Naomi glanced at Sadie and smiled. "I didn't think they could do it, either," she said.

Sadie wasn't sure about this, she glanced nervously around the circle. "I don't want to cause any trouble..."

Anna interrupted her. "It's no trouble. We don't want to see you miserable now, do we?" she said, and the others shook their heads.

"Your carpenter seemed nice. His name's Lloyd, isn't it? Lloyd Fehr. His *mamm's* called Melanie, am I right?" Rebecca asked.

"That's right. He's done a good job, and that dog he brought with him – just adorable," Anna said.

Sadie smiled at the thought of Fletch and how he had come running over to her to have his ears ruffled. She liked Lloyd very much, even though they had barely spoken, but she could only imagine what he must think of her now he had heard the revelation about her being promised to Samuel Miller.

"You could do worse than him," Rebecca said, looking pointedly at Sadie, who blushed.

But Sadie shook her head, feeling suddenly terribly embarrassed. Here she was, holding the son of Naomi and Aaron. They had found love, they had found one another, and they were happy. Naomi had her cake-making business and a beautiful *boppli* to call her own. Sadie had only a few hens and ducks and a vegetable plot. It was hardly an attractive proposition, even as she knew she should have more faith in herself.

Sarah Beiler seemed to sense this lack of self-worth, and she gave Sadie a reassuring smile. "I'm sure he'd like to get to know you. Why don't you talk to your *daed*? Tell him you just don't think Samuel Miller's right for you. But Lloyd... He's not courting, and I don't know anyone who's caught his eye – except perhaps you, Sadie," Sarah said.

Sadie blushed an even deeper shade of red. She did not think she had caught Lloyd's eye. Far from it, in fact. They had met in a chance encounter, and it was only Fletch who had caused them to linger in one another's company a little longer than they might otherwise have done. It was a nice idea, but not one Sadie felt she could entertain.

"I don't know... it's not something I've thought much about. Anyway... I need to speak to my *daed*. He and Dwain Miller have it all thought out, or so they say. I feel like a pawn in a game," she said.

The other women shook their heads.

"You poor dear," Susanna said, and Sadie's *grossmammi* looked anxiously at her.

When the quilting circle had come to an end, they bid goodbye to Anna, who assured Sadie she would do her best to help her.

"We won't let this turn out the wrong way. We did it once with Naomi, we can do it again," she said, seeing Sadie and her *grossmammi* out of the door.

They walked across the neat garden and out onto the road, where Mary turned to Sadie and put her arms around her.

"Oh, Sadie, don't be despondent. Your *daed* means well, even if he's not going about things the right way. I'll talk to him. I'll help you to make him understand. But don't dismiss Lloyd out of hand. You might be surprised at how he feels," she said.

Sadie doubted it. The attentions of a dog and a few kind words were hardly a basis for courtship. She felt miserable and would far rather have been left to continue in her own way and without her *daed* interfering.

"I don't know. Perhaps... but what does it matter? My *daed's* going to have things his way and that's that," Sadie replied.

Mary sighed and put her arm around Sadie, who was fighting back the tears. She had tried so hard not to cry and had hoped the quilting circle would allow her the chance to think of something different. But the discussion of marriage and seeing Naomi so happy with Lucas had only served to remind Sadie of all she was yet to gain, and that she may never do so.

"We'll see about that, Naomi. Don't you worry, all right?" Mary replied.

Sadie was not ready to return home just yet and thanking her *grossmammi* for her kind words, she made her way instead towards the creek, where she hoped to sit by the water's edge and think.

"There's a lot I need to think about," she told herself, as now she made her way down the path towards the water's edge and wondered what would happen to her if her *daed's* plan was to come to fruition... It did not fill her with joy, but quite the opposite.

CHAPTER SIX

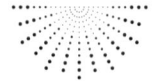

The heat of that summer's afternoon was about to break. Sadie could smell it in the air. Clouds were gathering, and it seemed her quiet contemplation was about to be disturbed by the coming of a storm. There was no time to run home, for the path led across the open cornfields and she would be soaked to the skin. Sadie could not afford to catch a cold – she had too much to do, and instead, as the first drops of rain began to fall, she took shelter under the boughs of a large oak tree, the branches of which provided her with shelter from the worst of the rain, that now fell in sheets, bouncing off the surface of the water in the creek, and running in rivulets across the dry ground.

What a storm, she thought to herself, as a rumble of thunder echoed all around her.

It had been coming for some days, rising on the horizon and threatening its presence. Sadie enjoyed storms. In the winter, she would stand at the parlor window and watch them rolling over the prairie. But being caught out in one was different, and now the rain was dripping from the branches above her and running down her neck.

"Perhaps I should just make a run for it," she said to herself, torn between the certainty of a soaking and the thought of remaining beneath the uncertain protection of the oak tree for perhaps several hours to come.

But as she contemplated her decision, Sadie heard a noise. It was a dog barking, and she looked up and peered through the gloom of the trees. There it was again, a high-pitched bark, like a cry for help.

"Good dog, come here?" she called out, and she half imagined – half hoped – it would be Fletch who would appear, followed by Lloyd.

But the dog that appeared was not Fletch, and there was no sign of Lloyd with him. The dog was a golden retriever, its fur was matted and muddied and it wasn't wearing a collar. It stopped at the sight of Sadie sheltering under the tree and barked.

"It's all right, come closer," she said, holding out her hand to the dog, who shook itself of the rain and came bounding towards her.

Sadie was already wet – the tree offering little by way of protection from the elements – and when the dog jumped up at her and put its muddy paws all over her dress, Sadie knew there was little point in trying to shelter any further.

"Where are you from? Where's your owner?" she asked, imagining that at any moment, the dog's owner would appear from the trees and call it back.

But there was no one around, and it seemed the dog was on its own – lost or escaped from somewhere.

No collar, no identification tag, just a dog that found me, Sadie thought to herself, knowing it was a strange thing indeed.

She had never encountered a stray dog before, and it seemed the dog was only too happy to see her. It barked again and pawed at her, lolling out its tongue and gazing up at her with wide eyes. Sadie smiled.

"I don't know about you, but I'd like to get back inside and get warm and dry," she said, even as she imagined the dog would run off as soon as she walked towards the path leading away from the creek.

But to Sadie's immense surprise, the dog followed her. It seemed fearless and quite happy in her company. Sadie thought back to Fletch and how he had enjoyed having his ears fondled. She turned to the retriever and did the same, wondering what its name was.

"I don't know what to call you. You must have a name. Someone must own you," she said, reminding herself not to get too attached to an animal that was surely missing from its true home.

She hurried on up the path, hardly noticing the rain, which was falling heavily and bouncing off the path.

"I could call you... Bram – like Abraham, but shorter. Bram, yes, I like that," Sadie said, and the dog barked as though in agreement.

They had reached the edge of the cornfields now and emerged onto the road. The sky was still an inky black, and thunder rumbled menacingly around. A flash of lightning lit up the sky, and the dog whimpered.

"It's all right, Bram. We're nearly home. Stay close now," Sadie said, as they hurried along the road.

Bram followed Sadie through the gate into the small-holding. If anything was enjoying the rain, it was the vegetables, which had not seen rain for several weeks. The water butts would be full, and Sadie groaned at the thought of all the weeds which would sprout up after the ground had been soaked by the storm.

"This way, good dog," Sadie said, as she hurried up the steps of the porch, relieved to be out of the rain.

The dog sat down on the porch and rolled onto its back. It was soaking wet and muddy. Sadie could only imagine what her *daed* would say when he saw it.

"We need to get you dried off, then I'll give you a bath later on," Sadie said.

The porch served as an extension of the shed where Sadie stored her gardening tools. She had some old hessian sacks there, left over from the previous year's potato harvest. One of these served to rub down the dog, who stood obediently as Sadie dried him off. His fur was all matted, and it seemed he had been outside a lot longer than just in the moment of the storm.

"Where have you come from?" she asked, but the dog only looked at her and barked.

She smiled and beckoned it to follow her into the house. She opened the door into the parlor. Her *daed* was sitting fast asleep in an armchair by the stove, but as the door opened, he sat up and looked at her, then looked at the dog.

"Sadie, you're wet through," he exclaimed, as Sadie closed the door behind them.

"There's a storm raging, *Daed*. Didn't you hear it?" Sadie asked, for the rain was drumming on the roof, and as if to prove her point, a flash of lightning lit up the dark sky through the window.

"I've slept right through it, but... what's this?" he asked, pointing at the dog, who was now sniffing at the rug.

"I found him by the creek. He's not got a collar or a tag. I don't know who he belongs to," Sadie said.

Her *daed* shook his head. "You can't bring him here, Sadie," he exclaimed, but Sadie's mind was already made up.

"What was I supposed to do? Leave him outside in the pouring rain? I couldn't do that. No, he can stay here. I'll find out who owns him in the morning. He'll be all right. I've got some tins of chuck steak in the pantry to feed him with," she said, as the dog sat down on the rug and rolled onto his back.

Sadie's *daed* shook his head, but he made no further protests, and Sadie had soon set down a dish of chuck steak and a bowl of water for the dog, who ate hungrily. Thinking about it she could feel his ribs when she rubbed him down. How long was it since he had eaten?

Sadie sat on the rug next to him, stroking him and fondling his ears. Bram looked up at her and barked.

"You've certainly made a friend there," Leroy said.

Sadie laughed. "I'm glad. He's beautiful – well, he will be once I get him cleaned up. I'll heat some water and bathe him in that old copper tub," she said, even as her *daed* began to object.

"Now, don't get ideas into your head, Sadie. He'll have to go back to whoever owns him first thing tomorrow. I can't have a dog here, and..." he began, but he was suddenly seized by a violent coughing fit, which doubled him over as he spluttered and choked.

Sadie felt her heart clench, how she hated to hear him in such distress.

CHAPTER SEVEN

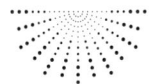

Sadie hurried to fetch a glass of water, knowing there was little she could do but try to make her *daed* comfortable. She rubbed his back and held the glass up for him to drink from.

"It's all right, *Daed*. Why don't you go to bed? I'll help you get upstairs," Sadie said, and her *daed* nodded.

"These coughing bursts are getting worse. Oh, Sadie... I don't know what's wrong with me, and I've asked Samuel Miller to come round tomorrow. I thought the two of you..." he began, but Sadie interrupted him.

"We'll talk about it in the morning, *Daed*. Right now, you need to go to bed and rest," she said, adopting a firm tone.

To her relief, he allowed himself to be led upstairs and put to bed. His breathing was still labored, but he was comfortable now and smiled at her as she kissed him goodnight.

"I don't know what I'd do without you, Sadie," he said, and she smiled back at him.

"You don't have to. Now try to get some sleep and call me if you feel worse. I'll run for Doctor Yoder... if need be," she replied.

He nodded, and Sadie realized just how unwell he must be feeling, given he no longer objected to the doctor's presence. Sadie bid him goodnight and made her way back downstairs. She was tired, but she wanted to wash Bram, and now she set about heating water on the stove before pulling out the old copper tub and filling it with soap suds. The dog was asleep on the rug in the parlor, and Sadie reminded herself she would need to wash the rug, for Bram had covered it in dirt.

"Come on now, let's get you cleaned up," she said.

The dog looked up and gave a short bark. Sadie smiled and beckoned for him to follow her. He got up and lumbered across the parlor. To her surprise, Sadie now noticed he was limping. Out in the darkness and with the rain pouring down, she had not noticed his limp, but there it was, his front left leg held up, as though it was painful to walk on.

"What have you done?" she asked, stooping down to look at the dog's paw and wondering if he had perhaps stepped on a thorn.

When she checked she could see a deep gash in the pad. Sadie was fearful that the dirt the dog was caked in would cause an infection.

"Into the bath with you," she said, pointing at the copper tub.

What followed was as much a bath for Sadie as it was for Bram. She was soaked from head to toe – her clothes having only just begun to dry after coming in from the storm. Bram seemed to enjoy his wash, and Sadie had to change the water several times for it became as black as the clouds outside, but by the time they were finished, Bram was the color he was supposed to be, and Sadie had dried him with a large towel so that his fur became fluffy and a much lighter golden color.

"Let me look at your paw a little better," she said, and to her surprise, Bram held out his paw and stood patiently as she examined it.

The wound was deep. Sadie brought bandages from her own first aid kit and bandaged Bram's paw before settling him down on a different rug to the one he had dirtied earlier on and which now she rolled up for washing another day.

"There now, you go to sleep. I've done my best for you," she said, sitting next to him and stroking him.

Sadie really did love dogs, and Bram moved to put his head on her knee, looking up at her with wide eyes as she stroked his nose.

"What a good dog you are," she said.

She could hear her *daed* coughing, and she wondered whether to take him some more water. He would only say she was fussing over him, but the more he coughed, the more anxious Sadie grew.

"I just wish he'd get better. I've got to fetch Doctor Yoder tomorrow. He'll know what to do," she said to herself, for her mind was now resolved.

She thought of her *daed's* words about Samuel Miller, and how he was planning to call on them the next day. What would she say to him? What would he expect of her? If their first encounter had been awkward, the second was hardly going to be any better.

"What would you do?" she asked, but Bram was already snoring gently on the rug. Sadie yawned. It had been a long day, and the discovery of Bram had brought with it a great deal of extra work. Her *daed* had stopped coughing now, and Sadie wondered if she, too, could get some rest. But as she rose to her feet, Bram opened his eyes and whimpered.

"Oh, what's wrong? That didn't sound good," she said, as Bram now rolled onto his back and held up his paw.

"Is it hurting you? I hope it's not got infected," she said, reaching out and taking Bram's paw gently in her hand.

It felt warm to the touch, and Bram gave another whimper and whined.

Infection... oh, dear. I don't know what to do about that. There's no vet in Faith's Creek, but... oh, didn't Lloyd say he wanted to be a vet? Sadie thought to herself filled with a sudden hope.

Just then, her *daed* started coughing and a cry came from his bedroom above.

"Sadie... I can't... breathe," he called out, and Sadie leaped to her feet and rushed up the stairs.

Her *daed* was trying to sit up in bed and gasping for breath. Sadie hurried to his side and put her arms around him, rubbing his back and holding him up so that his breathing grew steady once again.

"You shouldn't try to move. I'll go and fetch Doctor Yoder," she exclaimed, panic now rising in her mind.

Her *daed's* condition was growing worse, but he shook his head, gasping for breath.

"No... your *grossmammi*, fetch her," he said.

Sadie was not about to argue with him. She was only glad to know he would accept help from anyone. She nodded and helped him lie back on the bed. Sweat was pouring from his brow, and she helped him drink some water before unbuttoning his night shirt and soaking a flannel she held to his brow.

"I'll go for her. She can sit with you. But in the morning, I'm fetching Doctor Yoder," she said.

Her *daed* gave no further argument, and whilst Sadie was anxious about leaving him, she knew there was no choice but to go and fetch her *grossmammi*. It was late now, and she hurried downstairs and snatched up her shawl. Bram was whimpering on the rug. She kneeled at his side and stroked his head.

"You poor thing, does it hurt a lot? I didn't realize. I'm sorry," she said.

The dog looked up at her with wide, mournful eyes. His spark was gone, and Sadie was certain the wound had become infected.

"I'll fetch my *grossmammi*. She'll know what to do. Then I can sit with you," Sadie said, as she fondled the dog's ears.

It had stopped raining now, but the wind was still strong, and as Sadie hurried out of the house and across the dark garden, she felt an overwhelming sense of despair. Her *daed* was getting no better, and now the dog was sick, too.

"What a mess," she thought to herself, as she ran down the road in the direction of her *grossmammi's* house. What would she do if she lost them both?

CHAPTER EIGHT

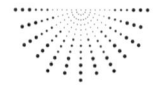

*L*loyd was washing the mud from Fletch after he had caught the dog rolling in the garden. Fletch always found the muddiest places and his fur was all matted.

"Don't you move from that mat," he warned him, ruffling Fletch's ears as he brushed him down on the porch.

"It was quite a storm last night, wasn't it?" Lloyd's *mamm* said, emerging from the house to bring him a cup of coffee.

The high winds had brought down a bough from their apple tree and it had broken part of the fence at the end of the garden. Lloyd was going to mend it, but he had some work to do that morning – work he had been putting off for some time.

"We're lucky it didn't take any of the roof off," Lloyd replied, wiping the last of the mud out of Fletch's coat.

"Speaking of roofs, are you going up to the Millers today? You said you would," Lloyd's mamm said.

Lloyd sighed. The Englischer, Dwain Miller, had asked him some weeks previously to look at the roof of one of his barns. The guttering had come loose, and some wooden panels needed replacing. Lloyd had agreed, but that had been before he had discovered Samuel Miller's interest in Sadie. He knew it was foolish to feel jealous – he barely knew Sadie, and if she was going to marry the Englishcher's son, then so be it – but despite this, Lloyd had still put off the inevitable.

"I suppose I'd better. I just... well, it doesn't matter. Come on, Fletch, let's get going," Lloyd said, and the dog barked and leaped up at him.

"He'll get you all muddy with his paws, Lloyd," Melanie called out, but it was too late.

Lloyd's trousers were covered in muddy paw prints, whilst Fletch looked up at him excitedly, as though he thought it was time for a walk.

"I can tell it's going to be a long day," Lloyd said, picking up his carpentry bag.

The Millers owned a large farm on the edge of Faith's Creek. Dwain Miller had come from Oregon to farm, though his idea of farming was more akin to moving large pieces of machinery around and letting them do the work for him. He was rich and treated Faith's Creek as an eccentricity, one he could exploit for his own ends.

"I was beginning to give up on you, Lloyd," Dwain said when Lloyd knocked on the door of the large, modern house a short while later.

"I'm sorry, Mr. Miller. I've had so many jobs to do recently. It feels like the whole of Faith's Creek wants a carpenter at the moment," he said.

Dwain nodded. "Well, you're here now. It's the barn over there. I need you to go up the ladder and replace those panels. Then attach the guttering back on. Can you do that?" he asked.

Lloyd *could* do that. He could do most anything he turned his mind to, and it was not long before he had a ladder up to the side of the barn and was climbing up to replace the panels. From the top of the ladder, Lloyd could see across the farm and over the prairie. The storm of the night before had cleared, leaving a bright, sunny day behind. Lloyd was thinking about Sadie, and whilst he knew he was a fool to do so, he simply could not help it.

"I'm meant to be seeing the egg woman this morning. I don't think I can be bothered," a voice from below said.

The repair to the gutter was at the angle of the barn so that the ladder was hidden from view to anyone at the front. Lloyd could see across the gable roof, and he spotted Samuel Miller, talking to one of the farm hands. He was a tall, broadly built man, dressed in sportswear and a baseball cap, and looking entirely out of place. Lloyd knew how much Samuel detested living in Faith's Creek, and now he wondered who the "egg woman," was supposed to be.

"It sounds like you don't have much choice in it," the other man replied.

"I'll play her along for a bit. It's always funny seeing these Amish girls led astray. They get all worked up over marriage. I'm not going to marry her. I don't know why my old man even suggested it. He's friends with her father or something. I don't know why he bothers with this place," Samuel replied.

Lloyd nearly dropped his hammer in shock at the realization of what he was hearing. Samuel was talking about Sadie and doing so in the most disparaging terms. It made him feel so angry he almost wanted to throw his hammer at the man. What was wrong with him?

"It's such a strange place, and you're right, the women are... well, they're not like other women," the other man said.

Samuel laughed. "You're right there. I can't wait to get away. I've nearly got enough money for a bond on a property down in Florida. I wish my old man would just give me the money, but he's got it into his head to make me work for it. Just a few more months, then I can get away. But I know one thing – I won't be taking the egg woman with me. Come on, let's get to work," he said.

They walked off across the farmyard. Lloyd shook his head in astonishment. He could not believe what he had just heard, and his stomach was twisted in knots. The thought of Samuel leading Sadie astray, leading her on, leading her into sin... Lloyd climbed down the ladder. Fletch was sitting in the sunshine – he had not run to Samuel Miller or barked a greeting.

"You know what he's like, too," Lloyd said, just as Dwain emerged from the house.

"You've done a good job. I've got more work if you want it," he said, handing Lloyd his payment.

"I'm pretty busy at the moment, Mr. Miller, but I'll try my best," he replied, though secretly he had vowed never to return to the Miller farm again.

He called to Fletch to follow him and hurried out of the farmyard and down the track leading back to Faith's Creek. Lloyd's mind was filled with the awfulness of what he had heard, and now he wondered what to do in response. He could not stand idly by and allow Samuel Miller to hurt Sadie in that way. But would she believe him? He had presumed she was happy with the arrangement, and the thought of breaking her heart filled him with sorrow.

"I just don't know what to do, Fletch," he said, and the dog barked and leaped up at him.

It was to the home of Anna Troyer that Lloyd went next. She had a chair she wanted mending, and when he arrived, Lloyd was surprised to hear voices coming from the parlor as Anna opened the door.

"Oh, I'm sorry, I didn't realize you had company. You did say this morning, didn't you?" Lloyd said, wondering if another meeting of the quilting circle was taking place and if he was about to encounter Sadie inside.

But Anna shook her head.

"I didn't realize I would be. You've got the right day, Lloyd. Come in. It's just Sarah and Mary. They've called in for coffee. Would you like some?" she asked.

Lloyd nodded and smiled. "You're very kind, *denke*. Is it all right for Fletch to come in, too?" he asked.

"Dogs are always welcome here. We've just been talking about a dog," Anna said, beckoning Lloyd to follow her inside.

In the parlor, Sarah Beiler and Mary Erb were sitting by the stove drinking coffee. A large seed cake stood on the table in front of them, with several slices cut out.

"Hello, Lloyd, is business good?" Sarah Beiler asked.

Lloyd nodded.

He liked Sarah Beiler – and her husband, Bishop Amos Beiler. She had a way of being kind to people just when they needed it, and Lloyd remembered her bringing a casserole to their house when he was a little boy and his *mamm* had been in bed with pneumonia.

"It seems to be. I've just been up at the Miller place fixing panels on the barn, now I'm here, and later on, I've got a cabinet to finish for Dwight Leabetter. I'm really pleased with it. It's made from a fallen tree by the creek," Lloyd said.

Sarah smiled. "I'm glad to hear it," she said.

"I've certainly heard the name Miller a great deal these past few days," Mary Erb said, shaking her head.

Lloyd thought back to the conversation of the other day at the quilting circle and of the revelation of Sadie's match with Samuel. He wondered if it was his place to say something now. Mary was Sadie's *grossmammi,* and it was clear she had little patience for the idea of Sadie marrying Samuel.

"Is Leroy still set on the idea of Sadie marrying Samuel?" Sarah asked.

Lloyd felt his face blush, and he turned away, looking around him for the broken chair.

"He said as much again last night when Sadie brought me in. He's in a bad way, and the poor dog she found... oh, it's just terrible. It's got an infected paw. She sat up with it all night whilst I looked after Leroy. Doctor

Yoder came this morning – we both insisted on it," Mary said, shaking her head.

Lloyd was confused. He knew nothing of a dog, though it sounded as though the poor creature was in terrible distress.

"He needs a vet, too. But there isn't one in Faith's Creek," Sarah Beiler said, shaking her head sadly.

Lloyd glanced up from the chair and was surprised to find Anna looking at him. She smiled and raised her eyebrows.

"You know something about veterinary medicine, don't you, Lloyd? You want to be a vet. Your *mamm* told me about all the studying you're doing," she said.

Lloyd nodded. He felt terribly embarrassed, as now the eyes of all the women rested on him.

"Well... I know a little about it, yes," he replied.

"Oh. Don't be so modest, Lloyd. Your *mamm* told me you study every night and you're nearly ready for veterinary school," Anna said.

Fletch barked as though in agreement, and Mary looked at Lloyd with an expression of relief.

"Will you come and look at the dog? Sadie found him by the creek. He's got no collar on him. She's bandaged his paw, but it's got infected, and... she's so worried about him," Mary said.

Lloyd could hardly refuse, and whilst he felt sure this entire conversation had been carefully managed, he was only too glad to offer his help and see Sadie again...

CHAPTER NINE

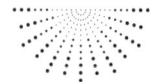

"What's going to happen to him, Doctor Yoder?" Sadie asked as the doctor came downstairs.

Sadie had been up all night. She was exhausted, but there was nothing she could do but keep going. Her *daed* was sick, Bram was whimpering on the rug, and it felt to Sadie as though her entire world was crashing down around her.

"It's not looking good, Sadie. Your *daed's* been hiding his illness for too long. He should've come to me the moment he started feeling unwell. He's coughed up a lot of blood in the night. I saw his handkerchief," Doctor Yoder replied.

Tears welled up in Sadie's eyes, and she sank into a chair by the stove and buried her head in her hands. Her *grossmammi* had stayed the night and had gone out to run some errands, promising to return later that day. Sadie was at her wits end, and now she looked up at the doctor and shook her head.

"He can't die, Doctor Yoder. I don't know what I'd do. I'd... oh, it's too awful. I couldn't imagine... and there's the dog, too. His paw..." she exclaimed, and fresh tears rolled down her cheeks.

Doctor Yoder put his hand on her shoulder sympathetically.

"I'm afraid I don't know about dogs. You need a vet for that. But... I think we might've got to your *daed* in time. I've prescribed some medicine for him, and with you as his nursemaid, well... I think he'll pull through. It's touch and go, though. A prayer and some medicine. That's what he needs," Doctor Yoder said.

Sadie nodded. She had been praying for her *daed's* recovery ever since he had first gotten ill. She would kneel at the end of her bed each night and pray that *Gott* would take the pain away. Now she resolved to pray harder and to ask *Gott* for the gift of life for her *daed* – as well as recovery. She wanted him to be the man he once was, strong and determined.

"I will. I will pray for him," she said, and Doctor Yoder nodded.

"That's what's needed now, Sadie. I'll call on you tomorrow, too," he said, taking up his medical bag.

Sadie saw him out. Bram was asleep on the rug, and not wishing to disturb him, Sadie made her way upstairs and knocked at her *daed's* bedroom door.

"Come in," he called out in a hoarse voice.

Sadie opened the door and stepped inside. Her *daed* was lying back on the bed. His face was pale, and his head was lolled to one side. She went over and kneeled next to him.

"Doctor Yoder says you're going to be all right. It'll take time, but you'll be all right," she said, wanting to give him hope, even in uncertainty.

"I... I don't know, Sadie. It all feels... too much," he replied, rolling onto his back with a sigh.

"You're weak now, but... you'll get better. I know you will," Sadie said, and she took his hand in hers and squeezed it.

"Perhaps... but it's you I'm worried about, Sadie. It's you I want to provide for. Samuel Miller... didn't he come to see you? He was supposed to. You've got to promise me, Sadie... promise me you'll marry him and..." her *daed* began, but Sadie shook her head.

"Don't get worked up about all this, *Daed*. If it's meant to happen, then, so be it," she replied.

This was not the time nor the place for an argument over marriage, even as Sadie had no intention of ever marrying Samuel Miller. But if the thought of her doing so was enough to give her *daed* some respite from his anguish, then so be it. Sadie knew he only wanted what was best for her, and whilst he had been misguided in knowing what that was, Sadie knew he would realize it eventually.

"You should go and see him. Talk to him. Tell Dwain I sent you," he said.

Sadie nodded. "I'll talk to him," she promised – anything to give her *daed* some peace.

"*Gut*. I just want to make sure you're going to be all right, Sadie. That's all I want. You know that, don't you?" he said.

Sadie nodded. "I'll be all right if you're all right, *Daed*," she replied and squeezed his hand.

Sadie was trying hard not to cry. She did not want her *daed* to know how much she was suffering in seeing him so unwell. She longed for things to be as they once had been, and for the happiness she had once known. She had spent so long distracting herself with her chores and her work on the smallholding, but now she had been forced to draw breath, and the terribleness of her situation seemed overwhelming.

"Just promise me you'll get married, Sadie. Promise me," he said.

Sadie nodded. "I promise, *Daed*," she replied, just as footsteps came from below.

"Sadie, I'm back," her *grossmammi* said, and Sadie squeezed her *daed's* hand again.

"I'll just be downstairs. Try to get some rest, *Daed*," she said, and she left the room, closing the door quietly behind her.

She was glad her *grossmammi* had returned, but from the landing, she was surprised to hear voices in the parlor.

"I'm sure I can do something," a voice was saying, and to Sadie's amazement, as she clattered down the stairs, she found Lloyd kneeling on the rug next to Bram.

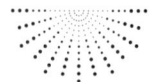

CHAPTER TEN

"*L*loyd, I... I didn't realize you were coming," Sadie said, as Lloyd looked up at her and smiled.

"He didn't realize he was coming, either." Mary chuckled. "I met Lloyd at Anna Troyer's house this morning and I explained about the dog and how we've been up all night with your *daed* and the poor creature. He said he'd come and take a look at the paw," Sadie's grossmammi said.

Sadie smiled. Despite all her troubles, she could not help but feel relieved at the sight of Lloyd kneeling next to Bram. He had brought Fletch with him, and the dog came running to her and sat looking up at her in greeting.

"No, Fletch, don't be pushy," Lloyd said, but Sadie did not mind.

She was only too happy to see him, and she ruffled his ears and kissed his nose.

"Oh, I'm so glad to see you. Do you think you can do something for him? Make him comfortable, at least?" she asked.

Lloyd was examining Bram's paw, gently unfurling the bandage. He had such a way with animals. Sadie watched as he stroked the dog's head, soothing him while peering down at the injury. "It's a little infected. Not badly, but enough to make him feel rough. You did a good job with the bandage and that's stopped it from getting any worse. I've got some ointment to clean it with and something to mix with his food to relieve the fever," Lloyd said, and he rummaged in his carpentry bag and brought out a bottle of ointment and a small bottle of pills.

Sadie was astonished at the way Lloyd now deftly went about his ministrations. The wound on Bram's paw was gently cleaned and re-bandaged before Lloyd took out some of Fletch's dog biscuit. He placed a single pill amongst a handful of them and held them beneath Bram's nose. The dog sniffed at them and then ate them

– pill and all. Lloyd stroked the dog's nose and looked up at Sadie with a smile.

"He'll be all right. I've got all the dirt out of the wound and those pills are enough to bring the fever down. I'll give him another one later. How's your *daed*? Has Doctor Yoder been to see him again?" he asked, rising to his feet.

Mary had gone upstairs to sit with her son, and Sadie and Lloyd sat down next to the stove. Fletch had gone to sit with Bram, and it was as though he were keeping watch over him in Lloyd's place.

"He's getting better – bit by bit. It's not going to be easy, though. He should've seen Doctor Yoder months ago. At least now, he's got a tonic to take and the doctor's coming back tomorrow. I'm really grateful to you for coming over too," Sadie said.

"When I heard about the dog, I had to come. I wanted to come... I wanted to help you," he replied, blushing slightly as he spoke.

Sadie smiled. She was glad he had done – very glad, indeed.

"You're very kind. You were amazing. The way you took care of him," she said, glancing down at Bram, who was sleeping peacefully with Fletch at his side.

"Well... I knew it was an infection, and I've read up about it. The wound needs to be thoroughly cleaned. That's the mistake a lot of people make. They only clean it partially. It needs to be thoroughly cleaned, and the dirt and any infected flesh debrided... got rid of. Then the bandage protects the open wound from getting any dirtier. If you don't do that, the dirt stays in and the bandage keeps it covered over. He'll be all right, though. Where did you find him? I couldn't see a collar on him," Lloyd said.

"I was down by the creek when that awful storm blew up. I was soaking wet and about to run home when suddenly the dog appeared. I heard it barking and at first, I thought it might be Fletch, but then Bram – that's what I called him – appeared. He's got no tags on him, though, and he was so dirty and thin, I think he'd been out there for days. He followed me back, and that was that," she said.

Lloyd shook his head.

"I hope he's not been abandoned. You hear such terrible stories – dogs left on the side of roads or dumped somewhere by the owner. No one should take on a dog unless they know how to look after it," he said, and there was such force in his voice that Sadie looked up at him in surprise.

"You feel really strongly about animals, don't you?" she said.

Lloyd nodded. "I've always loved animals. They're easier than people a lot of the time. I don't know what I'd do without Fletch. He's my best friend. I couldn't be without him. It upsets me to see animals badly treated. But enough about me, what are you going to do with Bram?" Lloyd asked.

Sadie had not given the matter a great deal of thought. She had assumed they would find his owner easily enough, but now she was beginning to wonder... with no identification, no collar, and no idea of his real name, Bram was a mystery.

"I suppose... I'd like to keep him. If I could. He's a lovely dog, but I don't know... can I just keep a dog like that?" she asked.

Lloyd shrugged. "I don't see why not. He is a little thin and has a few cuts; he could have been mistreated. If no one comes looking for him... well, you're the one looking after him. He followed you home. He looks pretty content to me," Lloyd said, smiling at Sadie.

"*Denke* so much. I don't want to keep you. If you've got other things to do," she said.

Lloyd shook his head. "I've got nothing I'd rather be doing. Besides, you look like you could use the company. It can't have been easy – last night, I mean. Taking care of your *daed* and Bram at the same time," he said.

Sadie felt tears welling up in her eyes, and she pulled out her handkerchief and dabbed her cheeks.

"I'm sorry... I don't mean to get upset. You must think me terribly foolish," she said.

Lloyd shook his head. "I think it's the natural response of anyone who's going through what you are. You're *daed's* ill, you've got so much responsibility, you're trying to hold it all together," he said.

Fletch came over to Sadie and put his head in her lap.

She smiled at him through her tears and ruffled his ears.

"He knows just what to do, doesn't he? You're very lucky to have him," Sadie said.

"He takes good care of me. You're right – he knows just what to do and when to do it," Lloyd replied.

"Shall I... make us some coffee?" Sadie asked, rising to her feet.

Lloyd smiled and nodded. "I'd like that," he replied.

The two of them sat for the rest of the evening drinking coffee and watching over Bram. Mary was upstairs with Sadie's *daed*, and Sadie felt as though she could at last relax. With Lloyd and Fletch there, she felt safe, and she was grateful to them both for what they had done.

"You must've wondered what you'd walked into at the quilting circle the other day," Sadie said, for she remembered how swiftly Lloyd had left after the other women had arrived.

"It was a little strange, I'll admit," he replied, shaking his head, and laughing.

"They're *gut* people, though. But I don't think I'll be finishing my blanket anytime soon. I couldn't get the stitching right and Naomi must've threaded my needle a hundred times," Sadie replied, laughing at the reminder of inability.

"But you've got other talents – keeping chickens is no easy matter, and neither is growing vegetables – not well, at least," Lloyd said.

"I like to sing, too," Sadie said.

"I'd like to hear you," he said, and Sadie blushed.

"Oh, I don't know…" she began, but Lloyd insisted.

"I'd like it if you would. I love to hear singing. It's so… relaxing," he said, and Sadie smiled and sat down on the chair near the stove where they kept the Ordnung.

"I could sing *Gott Be with You*," she said, and Lloyd nodded.

"I'd like to hear it, and the moon's so big and full tonight. It seems the perfect thing to sit and look at it and listen to your lovely voice," he replied, glancing out of the window.

Sadie got up and took his hand leading him out onto the porch where they both sat on the swing seat. She began to sing and was so pleased to see the look of awe in his eyes. She let her voice rise and soar and her heart did the same.

"That was beautiful, Sadie," he said, and Sadie blushed.

"It's just... well, I suppose I've always loved singing," she replied, feeling suddenly shy beneath his gaze.

"But... you're not just good... you're... it was perfect," he said.

"I can see the music. It's hard to explain. I just see it and my voice just seems to find the note. I don't have to think too hard about it. It just comes naturally, that's all," she said.

Lloyd nodded.

They sat and talked for another hour and at the end of it, Mary came out of the house.

"I'm going to go now, Sadie. It's getting late and your *daed's* settled. You might want to sit with him, though," Mary said.

Sadie nodded. She was prepared to sit up all night, even as she had barely slept the night before.

"All right, I'll go up. I... I don't want to keep you, Lloyd," she said, but Lloyd shook his head.

"You're not... and... well, I'll gladly stay with you, if you'd like me to," he replied.

Sadie did want him to. She glanced at her *grossmammi*, wondering if she would object if she would think it improper, but on the contrary, Mary smiled and nodded her encouragement.

"It would be good for you to have some company. If Leroy wakes up, I'm sure he'd be pleased to find Lloyd keeping you company. All right, I'll be back in the morning, and I'll bring Doctor Yoder with me," she said.

Sadie walked her to the gate, followed by Fletch, who stood at the gate and watched as Sadie's *grossmammi* made her way home.

"He's always looking out for people, isn't he?" Sadie said, turning back to Lloyd, who had gone to check on Bram.

"I think dogs know. It's like a sense they have. They're so intelligent – well, most are. Some just get stuck down rabbit holes," he replied, laughing, as Bram stirred from his sleep.

"How is he?" Sadie asked.

"He's doing all right. Do you want to see to your *daed*?" Lloyd asked.

Sadie nodded. She fetched a jug of water from the kitchen and buttered two slices of bread which she spread with jam. Her *daed* needed to eat something and if he was awake, she hoped to persuade him to do so.

"Would you come and sit with us?" she asked, as she emerged from the kitchen a few moments later.

"If you're sure. I don't mind just sitting down here," he said, but Sadie was sure.

"I'd like it if you did," she said, and the two of them made their way upstairs, followed by Fletch.

Sadie's *daed's* bedroom door was open, and a lamp was burning on the bedside table. She stepped inside, followed by Lloyd, and found her *daed* lying on the bed with his eyes closed. His breathing was better now, and he looked up and gave a weak smile.

"Oh..." he said, noticing Lloyd behind Sadie.

"It's Lloyd, *Daed*. He came to look at Bram's paw. I asked him to come up and sit with us. I've brought you some bread and jam. Would you like to eat something?" she asked.

Leroy nodded.

But as he sat up in bed, Fletch scampered forward and climbed up next to him.

"Fletch, no, don't do that..." Lloyd exclaimed, but Fletch was burrowing into the sheets and making himself quite at home.

Sadie was worried her *daed* would grow angry, but to her surprise, he smiled and ruffled the dog's ears.

"You're a bold one, aren't you?" he said.

Sadie smiled. "He likes it when you do that," she said, as Fletch curled up next to her *daed*.

It was as though he sensed just what was needed, and now he did it. Sadie glanced at Lloyd, who stepped forward to introduce himself properly.

"I'm pleased to meet you, sir," he said, and Leroy looked up and smiled.

"I'm pleased to meet you, too, Lloyd, and I'm glad you've brought this beautiful creature, as well," he replied, fondling Fletch's ears as Sadie sat down next to him, thankful for the hope she now felt in her heart.

CHAPTER ELEVEN

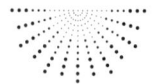

Sadie, Lloyd, and Fletch remained at Leroy's bedside for the rest of the night. He ate the bread and jam, drank a little water, and slept until dawn. Fletch was a calming influence on them all, and Sadie nodded off several times – despite her *daed's* snoring. When the first rays of dawn came, she looked over at Lloyd who was dozing in a chair at the end of the bed. Fletch raised his head and cocked it to one side.

"Did you sleep well?" Sadie whispered, fondling the dog's ears.

Lloyd opened his eyes and looked around him as though he had forgotten where he was for a moment.

"Oh, is it morning?" he asked.

Sadie nodded. "It's still early, but... I'd better go and see to the chickens and ducks. They'll be wondering where their food is," she said, and she rose to her feet.

Fletch jumped down to follow her, and her *daed* stirred and opened his eyes.

"Sadie?" he said, and Sadie smiled at him.

"It's early morning, *Daed*. I'm going to feed the chickens and the ducks. Then I'll bring you some breakfast," she replied.

Her *daed* nodded and yawned. Lloyd rose to his feet and called for Fletch to come down off the bed. Leroy looked sorry to see him go.

"Would you bring him back another time?" he asked.

Lloyd nodded. "I'll leave him here if you like. I can get a few jobs done and then come back," he said, glancing at Sadie, who smiled.

"I'm sure we'd all like that. Let's go and check on Bram," she said, and she led Lloyd from the bedroom and down the stairs to the parlor.

Bram was still lying on the rug, but he looked up at them and barked. It was not the pitiful whine of the previous evening, but a sharp bark, clear and strong. Sadie hurried over to him and kneeled at his side.

"He's looking a lot better, isn't he?" Lloyd said as he came to join her.

"He certainly is. Oh, Lloyd... *denke*. He's so much better, isn't he?" she said, and Lloyd smiled.

"Just like your *daed*, too," he replied.

"You're right. He's so much better – and it's all thanks to you and Fletch," she said, and without thinking, she flung her arms around him and kissed him on the cheek.

She felt such relief at finding herself unburdened of her troubles, and whilst she had taken herself by surprise at her own exuberance, it seemed Lloyd was not offended.

"And Doctor Yoder. We mustn't forget him," he said, and Sadie nodded.

"And the power of prayer, too," she replied.

Having made Bram comfortable again, Sadie put on her shawl and filled a bowl of chicken feed from the store in the pantry.

"I suppose I'd better be going," Lloyd said, but Sadie caught his arm.

"Could I come with you? My *daed's* all right with Fletch and my *grossmammi* won't be long. We could try to find Bram's owner," she said, with a hopeful tone in her voice.

Lloyd smiled, he appeared flattered to be asked, and he nodded.

"I'd like that. I'm not sure where to start, but we could try asking down at the market. Someone might recognize Bram. I know, we could take him in a wheelbarrow. He can sit in it, and we'll wheel him along. Someone might recognize him," he said.

Sadie thought this was an excellent idea, and she straightened her *kapp* and put on her shawl whilst Lloyd checked if Bram was all right to stand. He had certainly livened up and eaten several biscuits before Sadie was ready. When she opened the door onto the porch, Sadie was surprised to see a large cooking pot by the steps. It had a note attached to it, and Sadie stooped down to open it.

Dear Sadie, I thought a pot of chicken soup might help you in the coming days. It's always a favorite of mine when I'm feeling under the weather. Take care – we're praying for you. Sarah Beiler, Sadie read.

"That's kind of them," Lloyd said, as Sadie picked up the cooking pot and brought it inside.

"People are kind, aren't they?" Sadie said, smiling at Lloyd, who was now carrying Bram in his arms.

"Let's get him into the wheelbarrow," he said.

With some difficulty, they settled Bram into a wheelbarrow which Sadie normally used for moving compost, and wrapped a blanket around him. He looked quite funny peering over the brim, and the two of them set off towards the market square, each with one handle in hand.

"Someone must know something about him. I just hope we don't find out... well, that he's been used cruelly. No collar, no identification... I just don't understand it," Sadie said.

"That's because you'd never treat a dog like that. Sometimes, it's good not to understand other people – if we did, we might end up like them. Part of me doesn't want to know who he belongs to. They might want him back," Lloyd replied.

"But do you think I could keep him? I don't know if I could," Sadie said, but she had already answered her own question.

Sadie would keep Bram if she could. She had always wanted a dog, and she was only too glad that this one had entered her life so unexpectedly. They were walking along the edge of a large cornfield where the road split in two, one way leading to Faith's Creek, and the other to Bird-in-Hand. As they approached the split, Sadie was surprised to hear the roar of an engine. It was a motorbike and as it turned the corner the rider pulled up. They were wearing a helmet, and Sadie had no idea who it was until a voice called out to her.

"Sadie, I was just coming to look for you," he said – it was Samuel Miller.

He removed his helmet and ruffled his hair. Sadie glanced at Lloyd, who turned away. She wondered what he was thinking.

"I thought you were supposed to call on me," she said, and Samuel nodded.

"I was... but other things got in the way," he replied.

They were hardly the words of a man with the hope of marriage in his heart. Sadie looked at him curiously.

"I don't understand. Did you want something?" she asked, thinking back to the last time the two of them had spoken.

"All this stuff about getting married. I don't think my old man thought it through. Him and your father – they don't know what they're talking about. I'm moving to Florida. I can't get married. I've got a bond on a property there, I'm going to open a bar and then a gym," he said.

Sadie's eyes grew wide. She felt an overwhelming sense of relief at hearing these words, even as Lloyd turned to her with an anxious look on his face.

"Are you all right?" he whispered, and Sadie nodded.

She stepped forward and fixed Samuel with a searching look.

"You never wanted to marry me, did you?" she said.

Samuel shook his head. "We're pretty different, Sadie. But I don't think you wanted to marry me, either. Did you?" he asked.

Sadie was too polite to express her true feelings, but she sighed and nodded.

"I don't think it would've worked. It was just my *daed*... well, getting the wrong idea," she said.

Samuel nodded.

"That's settled, then. We don't need to... see one another again. I've never liked this place. If I got married to anyone from here... well, they'd have to come with me to Florida. No way am I spending the rest of my life in Faith's Creek. It's just a boring backwater where nothing ever happens," he said.

Sadie was not about to argue, even as she felt Faith's Creek was anything but a boring backwater. It was her home, the place she had grown up in, the place where her roots were, and the place she wanted to remain in for the rest of her life.

"I'm sorry you feel like that, Samuel. It's important to be happy in the place you live. That's what I think, at least," she said.

Samuel shrugged. "You're Amish. It makes sense you'd want to stay here. But not me... I don't want to be here anymore. I want to go to Florida. I want to make money," he said, scowling, as he revved up the engine on his motorbike.

"Well... good luck to you," Sadie replied, for she could not imagine Samuel would ever be truly happy – however much money he made.

"Oh, and you can keep the dog," Samuel said.

Sadie glanced at Bram in surprise. Did he belong to Samuel?

"Is this your dog?" Lloyd exclaimed, and Samuel laughed.

"He's a farm dog, and he's always getting loose. There was a litter of puppies, they lived in the barn... they weren't mine. Some of the farmhands fed them. This one – they called him Amos – he was always running away. I've not seen him in weeks. You're welcome to him. Just don't leave him unleashed. He'll run away, for certain," Samuel said, and now he revved up his engine and rode off back down the road, leaving Sadie and Lloyd staring at one another in disbelief.

"Can you believe that?" Sadie exclaimed, but to her surprise, Lloyd nodded.

"There's something I wanted to tell you. But I wasn't sure how you'd take it," he said.

Sadie looked at him curiously.

In all the excitement of the previous days, she had found little time for thinking, but now she wondered if Lloyd's arrival had been more than a happy coincidence. Perhaps he had meant to come. Perhaps there *was* something he wanted to tell her. Her heart skipped a beat, and she placed her hand on Bram's neck, the dog turning to look at her expectantly.

"What is it?" she asked.

Lloyd turned red with embarrassment. "I was fixing some guttering for Dwain Miller. He had me do some odd jobs for him, and when I was up the ladder, I heard Samuel talking to one of the farmhands – another *Englischer*," he replied.

"Was he saying how much he hated Faith's Creek?" Sadie replied.

Lloyd nodded. "He was, but... he was talking about you, too. I didn't want to upset you by telling you what he said. I thought you wanted to marry him. At the quilting circle, well... everyone said... I must've misunderstood..." he replied.

Sadie nodded.

It made sense now. Lloyd had left before she had voiced her objections to marrying Samuel. He must have believed she actually wanted to marry the *Englischer*, and now she realized how that must have made Lloyd feel if his own feelings for her were growing.

"Oh... I think you did," she said, and Lloyd shook his head.

"I was foolish. I should've asked you about it. But... I thought you wanted to marry him, and then I heard what he said about you," he said, looking sheepishly away.

It was no surprise to Sadie that Samuel Miller might have said something unpleasant about her. He said unpleasant things about a lot of people – and about Faith's Creek in general.

"What did he say?" she asked, and Lloyd blushed even further.

"He called you... 'the egg woman', and he said he was only going to have you as a distraction," he replied.

Sadie laughed. Of all the insults which might be directed towards her, the title of "egg woman" was hardly the worst. She rather liked it, in fact.

"There're worse things he could call me. I quite like it – 'The Egg Woman' – I could name my business that. I'm a woman who sells eggs, after all," she said.

Lloyd looked suddenly relieved. "You're not angry with me, are you?" he asked.

Sadie shook her head.

She could not be angry with him – there was no reason for her to be angry with him. He had told her the truth, and there was no doubt in Sadie's mind it was the truth. She could almost hear Samuel saying those words and dismissing her as an idle distraction prior to his move to Florida. At least he had had the decency to inform her, even as she had shed no tears as to his impending departure. Sadie felt free – free of the burdens which had seemed set to overwhelm her.

"How could I be angry with you? I'm sorry you misunderstood. I never wanted to marry Samuel. It was my *daed's* idea. He and Dwain – Samuel's *daed* – thought up the idea between them. I know he was only trying to help. He just wanted to make sure I was looked after if... well, the worst happened," she said.

Lloyd nodded. "You will be, I'm sure. But don't think like that. Your *daed's* going to be all right. I know he is," he said.

Sadie smiled. For the first time in a while, she believed that. "Thanks in no small part to you," she replied, smiling at him.

If Lloyd could have blushed any further, his face would have turned blue. But Sadie was speaking the truth, and it was a truth she wanted Lloyd to hear. The past day had served only to confirm the burgeoning feelings in her heart. That first encounter with Fletch on the road had sewn a seed, and now that seed was shooting forth. Lloyd had proved himself – he was kind, caring, considerate, and bold. He had helped her in her hour of need and stayed with her when he could so easily have left. That was what mattered, and Sadie wanted only to get to know him better.

"I didn't really do much," he said, but Sadie shook her head.

"You were there for me when I needed you – you and Fletch. And now you know the truth... well, maybe we could start again," she said.

He looked at her curiously.

"Do you mean...?" he asked, and Sadie nodded.

"That day we met on the road. I wish I'd come with you on the walk. And when you were at the quilting circle, I wish I'd talked to you more, and when all this was going on, I wish I'd come to you first instead of waiting for you. But I'm so glad you came – you saved Bram, you helped save my *daed*, and you certainly helped me," she said, and now she held out her hand to him.

He took it and smiled at her. Sadie's heart skipped a beat, and Bram barked.

"We could take him to walk on the ridge now. We could go and get Fletch and race the wheelbarrow up there," Lloyd said, and Sadie smiled.

"I'd like that," she exclaimed, as they turned the wheelbarrow around and ran with it along the road.

Both of them were laughing, and Bram began to bark. Sadie could not have felt happier at that moment – her burdens were lifted, her *daed* was getting better, Samuel was gone, she had a dog to call her own, and Lloyd was...

Whatever the future might hold, she thought to herself, as she met his gaze with a smile.

CHAPTER TWELVE

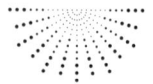

*T*he coming weeks were a whirlwind of activity. With the ministrations of Doctor Yoder, and the almost constant companionship of Fletch, Leroy began to get better. He grew stronger every day and was soon up and about, seeing to small jobs around the small holding. He would collect the eggs and feed the chickens, pull weeds up in the vegetable patch. Fletch followed him everywhere, and when Bram's paw was finally healed, he, too, followed Leroy around, displaying an unwavering loyalty.

"I never thought I'd see my *daed* so taken by dogs," Sadie said, shaking her head as she watched Fletch and Bram sitting next to Leroy, who was weeding amongst the cabbages.

"I'm just glad he's been able to help," Lloyd said, smiling at Sadie, who was sitting on the porch shelling broad beans.

Lloyd, too, was a constant visitor to the house. He would work there sometimes and was always on hand to help Sadie with any job she needed. It was a Thursday morning, and the two of them were due at Anna Troyer's house at eleven o'clock – Sadie for the quilting circle, and Lloyd to finish some odd jobs.

"They're both so loyal to him. I'm just glad the two of them get on. You never know with dogs, I suppose," Sadie replied.

"It's really interesting to watch them. I've been reading a lot of books on animal behavior lately. I find the psychology of it all so fascinating. I just wish I had the chance to put it all into use," he said, with a despondent tone.

Sadie knew Lloyd was feeling down about his prospects for veterinary school. The fees would be high, and whilst he was predicted to gain the highest grades in his science examinations, the prospect of what came next was dwelling on him. He had confided his fears to Sadie, and she had done her best to reassure him, but without money, it seemed like his dreams of becoming a vet were growing less likely by the day. It was not a traditional Amish trade. Usually, they used veterinarians from outside the district, but she knew it was Lloyd's Amish dream to be the veterinarian for Faith's Creek. It was his calling and she prayed that he could one day see it come true. His affinity for animals would make him so *gut* at it.

"You will do. Don't be despondent. You'll get there, I know you will," Sadie said, setting aside the bowl of broad beans and rising to her feet.

She held out her hand to him and he took it, giving her a weak smile as he got up.

"There's no shame in carpentry. It's a good profession. I just feel I've got something to offer. It's frustrating knowing so much but needing a piece of paper to prove it. I've read every book, I've seen every case around Faith's Creek – I've birthed sows, I've wormed cats, I've bandaged up a dog's paws, but it's not enough," he replied, shaking his head sadly.

"It will be. You've got to have faith," Sadie replied.

Lloyd gave a weak smile and nodded.

"Come on, let's go to Anna's house. I hope she's made banana bread again. It's delicious," he said, offering Sadie his hand.

They called out a farewell to Leroy, who promised to take care of the dogs until they returned and set off in the sunshine to walk the short distance together. Sadie was carrying a basket with the quilt she was making neatly folded inside. Over the past few weeks, Sadie had mastered the basics of stitching and managed to embroider her first quilt patch. It was nothing fancy – just red and green in a pattern – but she was proud of it and determined to finish what she had begun.

"I might invite my *grossmammi* for dinner tonight. You should ask your *mamm* to come. I can make buttered noodles – they're your favorite, aren't they?" Sadie said as they came to Anna's gate.

"It's good of you to try and cheer me up, Sadie. I'm sorry for being miserable," Lloyd said, and Sadie squeezed his hand.

"You're allowed to be miserable. We all are. But you're right, I am trying to cheer you up. You still need to eat, so why don't we enjoy it?" she replied.

To their surprise, it was Sarah Beiler who opened the door that morning. Anna was making coffee and the Bishop's *fraa* ushered them both in. The rest of the quilting circle had already arrived, and there was another surprise in the form of Bishop Beiler himself, who rose from a chair by the stove to greet them.

"Are you going to make a quilt, too, Bishop Beiler?" Sadie asked.

The Bishop laughed. "It's Amos remember? I can sew the words of the scriptures together, but I couldn't sew a thread to save my life. No, we've enough quilts in the house thanks to Sarah's efforts. No, it's Lloyd I've come to see. Sarah mentioned he'd be here, and you would, too, Sadie," he replied.

Sadie and Lloyd looked at one another in surprise. Sadie did not know why the Bishop should want to see them both, and she wondered if he was about to chastise them for their behavior. They had done nothing wrong, and whilst they had been spending a great deal of time together, their friendship had gone no further than that.

"We haven't done anything wrong have we?" Lloyd asked – clearly thinking the same as Sadie – but Amos shook his head.

"Not at all, no, it's about veterinary school, Lloyd," he said.

Lloyd looked at him curiously.

"I'm not sure I'm going to go, Bishop... sorry, Amos. It's so expensive and there aren't any scholarships. I wish I could, but..." he began, but Amos interrupted him.

"Did you know, the Hochstettler farm lost half a dozen ewes last year to illness, and poor Mary Hershberger doesn't know what to do with herself now her parrot's died? Then there are the working dogs – they're always getting scrapes and cuts, not to mention the horses. The trouble we have with horses... and the cattle," he said, shaking his head.

Lloyd looked confused, and he glanced at Sadie, who felt equally so.

"I don't understand. I'm sorry about it, but I can't be a vet if..." he began, but Bishop Beiler interrupted him.

"We're going to pay your fees, Lloyd. The community, I mean. If we want to preserve our way of life, we need to look after our animals, and the best way to do that is by having one of our own looking after them. But you're right, you can't just read a lot of books. You need proper training. There's the veterinary college in Bird-in-Hand. Your *mamm* tells me you're on course for the highest grades in your science exams, all taken at home."

Lloyd nodded. He had worked really hard studying at night.

"We'll pay for you to go to the veterinary college in Bird-in-Hand. That way, you're not too far away," he said, glancing at Sadie, whose eyes grew wide with delight and excitement.

Lloyd was staring at the bishop in utter disbelief. He pinched himself and shook his head.

"Do you really mean it, Bish... Amos? I can't... oh, it's too wonderful for words," he exclaimed, and turning to Sadie, he threw his arms around her and kissed her on both cheeks.

The ladies all applauded, and Lucas promptly woke up and began to cry.

"I think he's happy, too," Naomi said, beaming at Sadie, who knew this was an answer to her prayers.

Lloyd had been so despondent about his prospects, but Bishop Beiler's words and promise had brought with them the happiness he so deserved.

"I can't believe it. I'm going to be a vet. I promise I won't let you down, I won't let the community down. I'll study harder than I've ever studied before. I'll come top of my class, and I'll be there for every birth, every broken bone, every poor parrot – all of it, I promise," Lloyd exclaimed, and he jumped up and down on the spot, whooping with delight.

Anna brought out a seed cake, and they celebrated the happy news together. The carpentry jobs were quite forgotten – as were the quilts – and later on, Sadie and Lloyd returned to Sadie's house together, full of exuberance at the happy news.

"I'll come back every weekend. It's not far to Bird-in-Hand. Maybe you could come there and see me, too. I won't be able to take Fletch, will I? But he can come and visit with you and Bram. Could he stay with you?" Lloyd asked.

Sadie smiled. "We'll work out the practicalities once everything's sorted out. Don't worry," she said, and Lloyd smiled.

"I'm sorry. I'm just... so excited, that's all," he said, but Sadie shook her head.

"You've every right to be excited. I tell you what, why don't we take the dogs for a walk on the ridge? You can tell them the *gut* news, too," she said.

Sadie's *daed* was as excited as Sadie at Lloyd's news and he was full of congratulations for the would-be vet.

"I'm sure you'll be very happy, Lloyd. You work hard and that's admirable. I'm pleased Bishop Beiler's recognized that," he said.

Lloyd thanked him, and Sadie put leads on the dogs. It was a nice afternoon in early fall, and the leaves were beginning to turn red and golden on the trees. They would let the dogs off once they go up onto the ridge. Sadie took Bram's lead in her hand, leading the way, with Lloyd and Fletch following behind.

"There's so much I still need to learn," Lloyd said, as they walked up onto the ridge together.

"That's why you're going to veterinary college. You'll learn all the things a book can't teach you, and you'll get real-life experience with the animals," Sadie replied.

"You're so supportive. You don't... mind me going away, do you?" he asked, pausing on the ridge, and turning to her.

Sadie shook her head.

"You'll be back on the weekends, and I'll come and visit you. I'll look after Fletch," she replied.

He looked at her and smiled.

"I'm lucky to have you, Sadie, but... I'm sorry I've been so down these past few weeks. I wanted... there's something I need to tell you. Something I want to say," he said.

Sadie's heart skipped a beat, and she looked at him curiously. What was he going to ask her? She knew what she hoped he was going to say... The two dogs were sitting together in the long grass, and Fletch barked as, to Sadie's surprise, Lloyd sank down on one knee.

"Oh, Lloyd..." she gasped, as he took her hand in his.

"Sadie, I love you. And I want to ask you to marry me. You mean the world to me, and now I know I've got a future – the future I've always dreamed of – I want you to share it with me," he said.

Tears welled up in Sadie's eyes. This was what she had longed for, what she had hoped for, and all she now wanted.

"I will marry you, Lloyd. I love you, too. We can get married before you go to college. Perhaps I could get a job in Bird-in-Hand. My *daed's* so much better now, he could manage with Anna's and *grossmammi's* help. I could work in a shop or teach singing..." she said, as Lloyd got to his feet and put his arms around her.

"It doesn't matter. All that matters is that we're together. I loved you from that first moment – it was Fletch who made me realize. He's got a *gut* nose, hasn't he? I knew then, Sadie, and I know now. I love you, and I want to be with you forever," he said.

Sadie smiled. "Fletch and the quilting circle," she replied, and Lloyd laughed.

"They've got a lot to answer for," he said, and now he kissed her, and the two dogs came running to leap up at them and share their joy as they walked home hand in hand with a bright future ahead of them.

EPILOGUE

1 YEAR LATER

Sadie walked into Anna's home, her arms loaded down with quilting material.

"My goodness, look at you." Anna rushed over and took the bundle from her. "You look so *gut*, almost glowing." Anna kissed her cheek and put the bundle of material down in the center of the living room.

Sadie blushed, *should she say anything?*

Chairs were already arranged in a circle waiting for the rest of the members to turn up.

"How's your *daed*?" Anna asked. "I didn't call in this morning."

"He's doing great. He was talking to the chickens and ducks when I arrived. He says they are such *gut* company... I can't deny that, they were *gut* for me too."

"That they are," Anna said. "How is married life, eight months now, are you still excited?" Anna smiled and winked letting Sadie know she was teasing.

"Lloyd is a wonderful husband. Very busy with his studies and he still comes back to Faith's Creek to help out when an animal is sick. But he makes me feel special all the time. We are very happy." Sadie knew that she was grinning like a *kinner* in a sweet shop.

"Morning," a voice called and Sarah Beiler appeared in the room. "*Ack*, Sadie, you are looking well. It is *gut* to see you."

"You too." Sadie hugged Sarah as more members arrived for the quilting circle.

Soon they were working on their projects, drinking coffee, and eating slices of a beautiful and moist coconut cake that Sarah had brought with her.

"How are you finding the job?" Susan Bontrager asked.

"I'm loving it," Sadie said. She was working making quilts in Bird-in-Hand where she and Lloyd had found a small apartment to live in while he studied. It had all been a joy and the small place was paid for by Sadie selling quilts and occasionally working in a diner. The district helped by paying Lloyd's tuition fees and her *daed* even helped them out with money from the eggs.

Sadie missed her chickens and ducks but she had Fletch and Bram. The two dogs were the best of friends and great company. Sadie couldn't imagine that her life could get any better but it had.

"Why are you smiling so much?" Anna asked her.

Naomi Wittmer stood up and automatically adjusted the blanket over her son, Lucas, who was snoozing in his crib. Naomi walked over to Sadie and looked at her. With a smile, she shook her head and returned to her seat.

"What is going on?" Rebecca Kuhns asked.

"Have you told your *daed*?" Sarah Beiler asked.

Sadie grinned and nodded. "*Jah*, this morning."

"Told him what?" Anna asked. She was looking around the room as a chorus of ahs went around the circle. "What?" Anna asked.

"I have to thank all of you in this circle for my happiness," Sadie said.

"*Ack*, you don't need to thank us," Anna said still looking confused.

"It is for that reason that after I told Lloyd and my *daed* that I thought you should be the next ones to know."

"Know what?" Anna was back to her quilting while the rest of the women were looking on with smiles on their faces. Slowly, Anna put down her quilt and her mouth dropped open. "Really?!" she asked.

"*Jah,* Lloyd and I are going to have a *boppli!*"

Anna was across the room, Sadie stood up and was pulled into her arms. Life was *gut* and she was so lucky to have such a wonderful community to share her news with.

The rest of the morning was spent discussing *boppli's* names, whether it would be a girl or a boy, and who was going to finish the boppli's first quilt.

Sadie closed her eyes and listened to her friends and whispered a prayer of gratitude.

* * *

If you enjoyed this book you will love A Love to Heal Her Heart

CHRISTMAS BRIDES AND SEASONAL WISHES – PREVIEW

Faith's Creek, Pennsylvania.

The snow was mesmerizing, falling from the inky dark sky above and blanketing the garden in a pristine covering. The fields around the house appeared as a single expanse of white as far as the eye could see.

Beth Phillips stood at the window, looking out. She had been standing there for an hour or so, just watching the snow fall, thinking of nothing in particular. She liked winter, the warm fires and the cozy nights, the prospect of Christmas to come – though, for her, the season was always twinged with sadness.

It was December, and the first snows had hit hard that year, the ground frozen and the roads around Faith's

Creek icy and treacherous. But Beth had no reason to venture out, the smell of a casserole bubbling on the stove, and the crackle of logs on the fire kept her company as she waited for Isaac's return.

She sighed and pulled the curtain across the window, turning back into the parlor to check all was ready for her husband's arrival. As she did so, she caught sight of herself in the mirror by the porch door. Her long brown hair, always covered by her kapp when outside was hanging down over her shoulders, her wide blue eyes filled with tears.

"You need to cheer up before Isaac comes home," she told herself.

The house was pristine – there was no reason for it not to be. Each morning, after she bid goodbye to Isaac, sending him off to the blacksmith's store with a packet of sandwiches and a flask of coffee, she would make the bed, tidy the parlor, clean down the stove and work her way through a myriad of jobs which designed not only to ensure domestic harmony but also to provide distraction. The house was quiet. It was missing the one thing Beth desired more than anything else in the world: the sound of *kinner*.

The couple had been married for five years, and in those five years, Beth had conceived three times. Each occasion had been a cause for joy and celebration, and each had ended in bitter sorrow and disappointment. There were three *kinner* in Beth's heart, three *kinner* who should have been there now, their voices filling the house, which felt so empty. Every little sound was magnified, not only by the silence of that winter afternoon, but the silence Beth felt at being alone. Each *kinner* had been conceived in love, and each was lost, at rest with *Gott*, and leaving behind it a restless heart in Beth, and a deep sorrow, too.

She longed for a *kinner* to call her own, to hold, and to be a *mamm* to. The names of those three *kinner* were etched on her heart Elijah, Reuben, and Jonah – she thought of each of them every day, and now she glanced across at the mantelpiece, where always she kept three candles burning, one for each of the *kinner* she had lost. A tear ran down her cheek, and she scolded herself for allowing her emotions to overwhelm her. What sort of welcome would that be for Isaac, who was due home at any moment? She did not want him to see she had been crying, and she pulled out her handkerchief and wiped her eyes, just as footsteps on the porch announced his return.

"What a day, it's really come in bad," Isaac said, stomping his boots on the mat, so that the snow flew in white specs on the rug, melting as they hit.

"Oh, well, come inside and warm up. I've just put more wood on the fire. There's a casserole on the stove top, too. You'll soon warm up. How was your day?" Beth asked, coming to kiss him, and taking his hat and coat.

He was a handsome man, four years older than her, with dark hair and dark eyes, and a face which always seemed to smile. Beth loved him with all her heart, and that only magnified the sorrow she felt at not being able to give him the one thing she knew he desired above all else.

"It was all right, but we're going to be hard-pressed to finish the plow repairs for Daniel Graeber before Christmas. He wants the whole thing: stripping back, new parts – we might as well build him a new plow as repair the old one," Isaac replied, pulling off his boots and coming to sit by the fire.

Beth smiled, hoping he would not notice she had been crying. It was the same every day lately. As Christmas approached, she found herself thinking more and more about what they had lost. The house where they lived was close to the schoolhouse, and each morning, Beth would endure the sight of parents taking their little one there, the happy smiles on their faces, the shouts and cries, the laughter – she longed to share in all of that, for she had seen many of her friends become parents and knew the joy their *kinner* brought them.

"I'm sure you'll get it all done. Do you want a drink? Something hot, perhaps? I tried that recipe for mulled apple juice Sarah Beiler gave me. It's delicious," she said.

Isaac nodded. "What did I ever do to deserve you?" he said, smiling at her.

Beth blushed. She did not think herself deserving of Isaac. They had been childhood sweethearts, insepara- ble, and there had been little doubt in anyone's mind that they would marry. On that happy day, the world had seemed so full of possibility, and they had dreamed of starting a family together. But as the candles on the mantelpiece testified, such dreams had come to nothing. Theirs was a quiet house, and Beth longed for the one thing she could not have – a *kinner* of her own to fill the house with noise.

"I'll just see to the casserole," she said, retreating to the kitchen, as she felt fresh tears welling up in her eyes.

She ladled a cup of the mulled apple juice into a mug, setting it on the side, as she glanced out of the window across the darkening garden which backed onto their neighbor's yard. The Hochstetler's had built a snowman below their porch, with twigs for arms and pieces of coal running up its front as buttons, a carrot was stuck in for a nose, and pebbles made a smiling face and eyes, one of Moses Hochstetler's old hats was pulled down low over its head. She thought of the *kinner* at play, and she reached out and pulled the curtain quickly across the window lest her thoughts overwhelm her once more.

"Are you all right?" Isaac asked, and she jumped, not realizing he had entered the kitchen.

"Oh... I'm all right, it's just getting dark," she said, forcing her face into a smile, and turning to pass him the mug of mulled apple juice.

"And cold, I think we're in for a harsh winter," he said, taking the mug and holding it in both hands.

Beth nodded. She was not sure how much longer she could keep up her charade. Every day it grew harder to put on a brave face and say the right things. Inside, she was hurting, and she had no one but Isaac to confide in. He was so kind and worked tirelessly to provide for her. She felt guilty at the thought of adding to his worries, and she knew he was hurting, too. He did not speak of it, but the pain was clear to see. Sometimes, she would find him staring at the three lit candles, with a look of such sorrow on his face that it broke her heart to see.

"Last year was so mild, it's like the weather's making up for it. It's been years since we've had such snows here," Beth replied, taking the casserole off the stove.

"Maybe we should build a snowman, too," he said, smiling at her, and Beth laughed, remembering happier days when the winter would bring sledding and snow-ball fights.

The past was a far happier place than the present for Beth, and she would often allow her mind to wander, remembering fondly what had been.

"Let's eat," she said, taking two plates from the cupboard and ladling out the casserole.

Grab this amazing box set - 26 Christmas Brides and Seasonal Wishes for FREE with Kindle Unlimited

ALSO BY SARAH MILLER

All my books are FREE on Kindle Unlimited

If you love Amish Romance, the sweet, clean stories of Sarah Miller receive free stories and join me for the latest news on upcoming books here

These are some of my reader favorites:

The Amish Landscape

The Amish Family and Faith Collection

Find all Sarah's books on Amazon and click the yellow follow button

This book is dedicated to the wonderful Amish people and the faithful life that they live.

Go in peace, my friends.

As an independent author, Sarah relies on your support. If you enjoyed this book, please leave a review on Amazon or Goodreads.

ABOUT THE AUTHOR

Sarah Miller was born in Pennsylvania and spent her childhood close to the Amish people. Weekends were spent doing chores; quilting or eventually babysitting in the community. She grew up to love their culture and the simple lifestyle and had many Amish friends. The one thing that you can guarantee when you are near the Amish, Sarah believes is that you will feel close to God.

Many years later she married Martin who is the love of her life and moved to England. There she started to write stories about the Amish. Recently after a lot of persuasion from her best friend she has decided to publish her stories. They draw on inspiration from her relationship with the Amish and with God and she hopes you enjoy reading them as much as she did writing them. Many of the stories are based on true events but names have been changed and even though they are authentic at times artistic license has been used.

Sarah likes her stories simple and to hold a message and they help bring her closer to her faith. She currently lives in Yorkshire, England with her husband Martin and seven very spoiled chickens.

She would love to meet you on Facebook at https://www.facebook.com/SarahMillerBooks

Sarah hopes her stories will both entertain and inspire and she wishes that you go with God.

Made in United States
North Haven, CT
03 June 2023

37324103R00074